Green Boy and Stories of Other Creators

Green Boy and Stories of Other Creators

Anjali Khandwalla

Translated from Gujarati by

Pradip N. Khandwalla

PARTRIDGE
A Penguin Company

ISBN:	Hardcover	978-1-4828-1076-9
	Softcover	978-1-4828-1077-6
	Ebook	978-1-4828-1075-2

Partridge books may be ordered through booksellers or by contacting:

Partridge India
Penguin Books India Pvt.Ltd
11, Community Centre, Panchsheel Park, New Delhi 110017
India
www.partridgepublishing.com
Phone: 000.800.10062.62

Anjali Khandwalla (author)

Born in Mumbai in 1940 in a religious but liberal Gujarati family, Anjali Khandwalla has absorbed many influences. She went to New Era School in Mumbai where Gandhi and Tagore were icons, and all the religions were equally respected. An M.A. in philosophy and psychology at Wilson College, Mumbai, exposed her to Western thought. From 1967 to 1975 she lived in North America, where she taught courses on East-West Cultures and Quest of the Self at Vanier College, Montreal. She was a performing Indian classical vocalist who was trained by Ustad Niaz Ahmed and Ustad Faiyaz Ahmed of Kirana Gharana. She wandered in the towns and villages of South Gujarat to study its rich folk music, and she gave many concerts of these folk songs. Her interest in creativity has led her to conduct workshops on creativity and self-development for young people, married ladies, and social workers. She also has a strong interest in gardening, landscaping and interior decor. Her multi-faceted experiences have enabled her to explore a wide range of themes in her stories.

Anjali Khandwalla avoids pompous language and elliptical prose. Her prose is graphic and straightforward, and she frequently uses colloquialisms to spice her language. She does not use sex and violence as props. Yet her stories grip the reader because of their imaginative, offbeat content, finely etched Indian contexts, sizzling dialogues, a rich feel for human relationships and emotions, intriguing situations, and a flair for vivid descriptions. Some of her stories have been translated into several Indian languages, and she has earned many laurels: Critics Award—Sandhan, for the best book of Gujarati short stories of 1988; Gujarat Sahitya Sabha Award for her book 'Lilo Chhokaro' (Green Boy), for being the best book by a woman writer during 1984 to 1986; Gujarat Sahitya Academy first prize, 1986, for her collection of short stories ('Lilo Chhokaro'); and so forth. Besides 'Lilo Chhokaro', published by R. R. Sheth, from which the stories in this collection have been translated, she has authored another collection of stories titled 'Aankh Ni Imarato' (Edifices of the Eye). An English translation of the stories in 'Aankhni Imarato' and a few other stories has been published as 'Black Rose and Other Stories' by Sanbun Publishers.

Pradip N Khandwalla (translator)

Pradip Khandwalla, the translator, is a poet who writes in English and Gujarati. His literary works include three books of poems in English, namely 'Wild Words', 'Out', and 'Incarnations'. His 'Adhyatmik Krantina Phool' (Flowers of a Spiritual Revolution) consists of translations into Gujarati via English of over a hundred 'vachanas' of the Sharana or Veer Shaiva poets of the 11th and 12th century Karnataka in South-West India. The book got him the Gopalrao Vidhwans award of Gujarati Sahitya Parishad, Gujarat's premier literary body, and also an award given by Gujarat Sahitya Academy. Some of his English translations of Gujarati poems have been published in Indian Literature. Gujarat Sahitya Academy has published 'Vedanana Shikharo' (Peaks of Pain), his translation into Gujarati of Rilke's celebrated 'Duino Elegies'. His translation of a volume of Gujarati short stories of Anjali Khandwalla titled 'Black Rose and Other Stories' has been published by Sanbun Publishers. His volume of the translation into English of over 200 offbeat Gujarati poems, titled 'Beyond the Beaten Track: Offbeat Poems from Gujarat', has been published by Gujarati Sahitya Parishad. He has recently completed the trans-creation into Gujarati of some 300 poems originally written by him in English. This book is titled 'Manthan' (Churning). He has also published a book of critical essays in Gujarati.

Professionally, Pradip Khandwalla is an internationally known management scholar. He has an MBA from Wharton School, University of Pennsylvania and a Ph.D. from Carnegie-Mellon University, U.S. He taught at McGill University, Canada, for several years before returning to India in 1975. Until his retirement in 2002, he was a professor at Indian Institute of Management Ahmedabad where he held the L&T Chair in Organization Behaviour from 1985 to 1991, and served as the Director from 1991 to 1996. He has published well over a dozen professional books, including three books on creativity. One of his books on creativity has got DMA's best book of the year award, while another has got translated into Mandarin for distribution in China. One more book, 'Creative Society: Prospects for India' is under publication. He has been the recipient of the Lifetime Achievement Award of World HRD Congress for professional contributions.

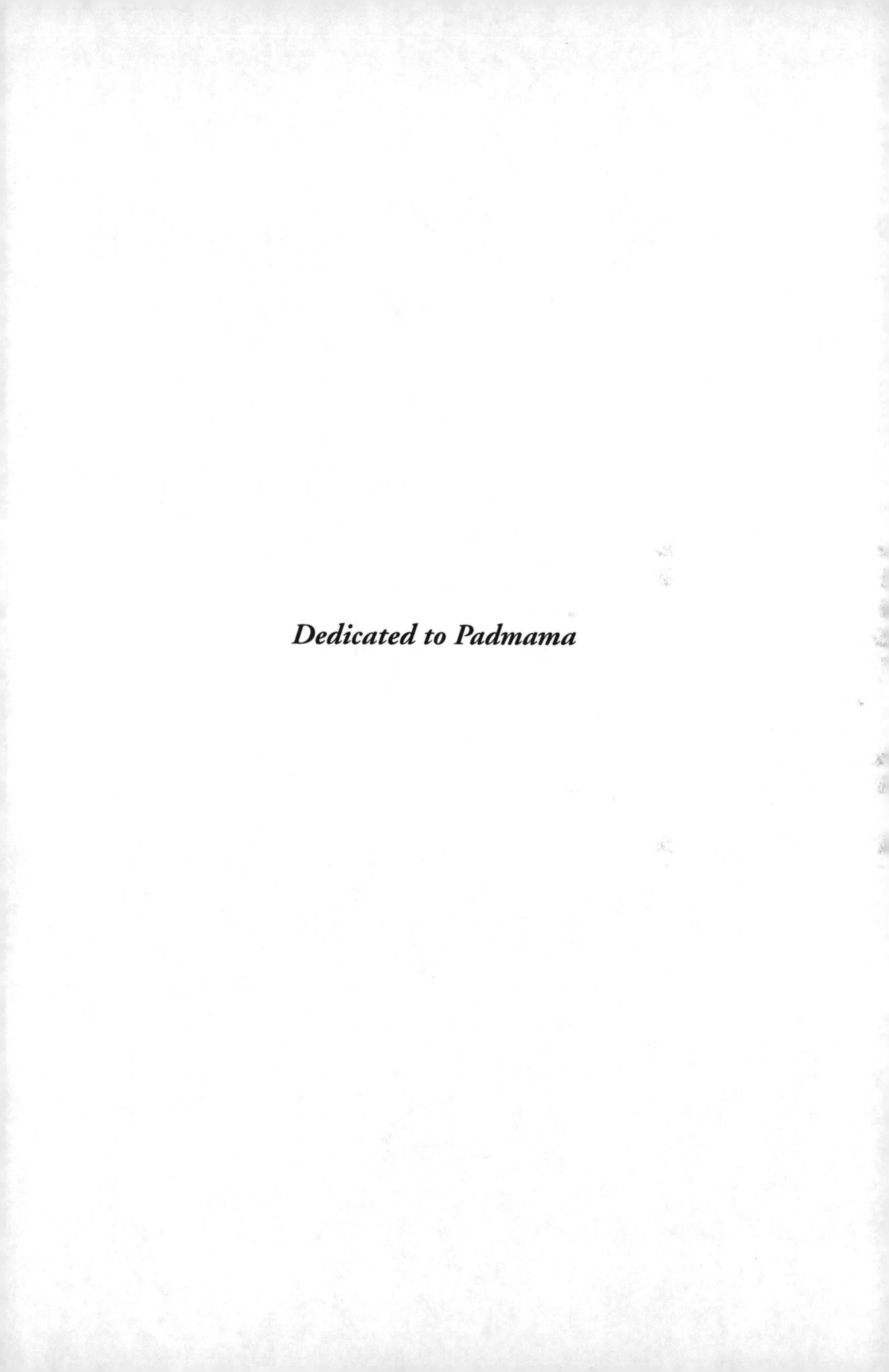

Dedicated to Padmama

Contents

Preface

This is a collection of eight stories about a special breed of young, resourceful, and energetic Indian men and women with a powerful commitment to their way of life. What is common between a youthful Canadian of Indian origin, who sets off for India to discover himself, and a lower middle class schoolgirl whose yearning for expressing herself through painting is choked by her parents? Or, between a botanist's son who can communicate with plants, an adolescent small town brahmin boy who loves to dissect dead animals, and a child-servant who wants passionately to be an innovative farmer? Or, between a youthful female mountaineer who lands herself into a world a thousand years in the future, a girl terrified of ghosts, and the son of a temple priest who is fascinated more by the rocks in riverside caverns than the idol in the temple? Passion for achieving something personally meaningful, persistence, humane sensitivity, and creativity are the traits common to these young Indians, in short supply in contemporary Indian youth. They fight pitched battles with their restrainers as well as with themselves for the freedom to pursue what moves them, and succeed in carving out astonishing niches. Multiply such dynamos a million-fold, and you have a vibrant, pre-eminent civilization.

The rearing in many Indian families and the teaching in most Indian schools are such that youngsters develop serious psychological blocks: excessive fear of failure that saps initiative; lack of confidence in dealing with the members of the opposite sex; an immobilizing conformity to social or parental norms; stereotyped perceptions of people of other communities; extreme dependency on 'elders'; social prestige driven choice of careers rather than a choice based on one's strengths and deepest yearnings, and risk aversion. The stories take head on the hang-ups from which many Indians suffer, and provide fresh ways of breaking out of these shackles. Although these stories are fictional, the discerning will find examples in real life of the kinds of people depicted in the stories and the struggles they go through to make their lives meaningful.

These stories paint a variety of Indian contexts. India is a collage of diverse lifestyles, and these stories vividly conjure them up. While one story is set in a lower middle class household, others are set in an upper class joint family, a Canadian Indian home, in the humble quarters of an abandoned countryside temple, in the farmhouse of an urbane scientist, and so forth. The characters are imaginary; but the stories seek to capture for the reader the vibrancy and diversity of contemporary India. The brief profiles of these stories are as follows:

The Green Boy is the story of Paurav, a boy with a 'green thumb' who can communicate with plants and can share their pains and pleasures. How does he prove to his botanist father, or, indeed to the rest of the world, that he can talk with plants? He sets out to prove this, and improvises many experiments. The story blends the scientific and the poetic, and the fusion extends our awareness of who we can be, for Paurav realizes that he can be both human and tree!

Peter: The author uses her teaching experience in Canada to advantage in weaving the adventurous tale of a Canadian young man of Indian origin who seeks to understand his Indian identity in the Himalayas at the feet of a spiritual master, in a Mumbai slum, and as a beggar on Mathura's streets. His offbeat experiences turn him into the principal of an uncommon school!

Ramadi is the story of a plain, lower middle class schoolgirl with a questing mind and a flair for painting. She struggles with the conservatism of her family and with her own personal hang-ups, reaches for the paintbrush with the help of an enthusiastic mentor, and exits from her prison into a wondrous landscape of freedom and colours.

Karna, the son of the chief priest of a small town in Gujarat has a problem: he loves to dissect carcasses to peer into their anatomy. But he runs smack into his parents' brahminical orthodoxy. He pushes off to the alien world of Mumbai to forge his destiny. He runs into a doctor who turns into a mentor and foster father. With luck and untiring effort he becomes a path-breaking expert on organ transplants. But his fame flings him back to his family, with nearly catastrophic emotional consequences.

The Great Ghost Hunt: Fear of the unknown often puts a full stop to enterprise. Overcoming terrors ingrained in childhood is every bit as heroic an enterprise as conquering a peak, and equally joyous. The author recounts the struggles of Avani to rid her mind of the fear of ghosts ingrained in her in childhood by the tales of a cook. Thereby, when she grows up, she rids others, too, of the spirits creeping about in the dark caverns of the mind.

Kaliyo: Child servants are still common in urban Indian homes. Kaliyo is one such, sent off out of dire necessity from his home in a Rajasthan village to work in a town in Gujarat. He finds a kindred soul his age: Shamli, his master's daughter. She helps Kaliyo, a peasant's son, to become an innovative farmer. Kaliyo gets beaten up at the height of his success, but stays the course and gives his farm a green shine.

Tufan is a lad who lives in a temple outside a village. He gets engrossed in clods and rocks because he can distil pigments from them. He seeks out a well-known painter in a city who becomes his mentor and customer. The grown up Tufan goes into the business of making and selling colours. But the entrepreneur's path is paved by thorny people. At the end there is a smile on the face of Tufan and his team, though their eyes remain wary.

Millennium Old Ahalya: A snowstorm in the Himalayas claims the life of a vivacious young mountaineer. A thousand years later, her frozen body is restored to life by a team of scientists. The people she meets are peace-loving but emotionally and physically anemic. She finds them amazing but intolerable, and the feelings are mutual. There is a titanic struggle, and the outcome is the renewal of the human race.

All eight stories have been translated from Anjali Khandwalla'a awards-winning book 'Lilo Chhokaro' (The Green Boy). Translating stories from Gujarati, or for that matter from any Indian language into English, poses many challenges because of differences in idiom, connotations of words, and sentence structure. The difficulties are compounded when the stories are written in a style full of forceful graphic images and allusions that sound fine in the original but clumsy in literal translation. The translator therefore abandoned any attempt at literal translation and trans-created them to read like stories written in (Indian) English—with enough of Indianness, but not to the point that the reader finds it awkward. Luckily, the translator had ready access to the author, and so it was possible to be reasonably faithful both to the original text and to the intended meanings of its phrases.

These stories have many strengths: lucidity; racy narration; eye-popping imagery; diversity of settings; memorable characters; a very positive message; and gripping story-content. Many young people as well as older people were enchanted with the stories in their original form in Gujarati. Those who read fiction in English may also find them memorable.

-Translator

ACKNOWLEDGMENTS

I owe a debt of gratitude to Anjali Khandwalla for painstakingly going through the first drafts of the translations of her stories and for making many useful suggestions. I am very grateful to Jitu Mishra for help in designing the cover pages of the book. I also availed of the help of Gayatri Parekh for this purpose. A number of persons graciously allowed their photos to be displayed on the cover page. These include Ashish Amin, Shama Desai, Jagdish Municha, Sreejit Nair, Saloni Shah, Shyamal Shodhan, Dharti Thaker, Prashant Trivedi, and Diti Vyas. I am grateful to Dia Mercado of Partridge Publications for clarifying many points connected with this publication.

Translator

THE GREEN BOY

"Pappa . . . Pappa . . . Pappa" squealed five-year old Paurav. He flew up the stairs to his father's study, pushed the door open, and entered it. "Get up Pappa, the tree is walking", he cried twice or thrice in a shrill, cracking voice. Eyes popping, he tugged with his little fingers at the collar of his Pappa, who was engrossed in writing. The father got up with a jerk, as if startled awake from slumber. Holding his father's fingers in a vice-like grip, Paurav dragged his father off to the living room on the ground floor.
"Look Pappa! He . . . is coming near me," Paurav said in joyous amazement. He pointed to a potted rubber plant kept in a corner. Dr. Mehta, one of the country's well-known botanists, stared at the plant and rubbed his eyes.
"Pappa! He wants to go out into the sunlight. He is telling me to take him out of this room."
"Paurav, a tree does not walk or speak—such things happen only in a story."
"But Pappa! Look . . . !"
"Come, let us go and meet Mithu Uncle." The father grabbed Paurav's arm. Paurav was quite well behaved and rather mature for his age; but that day he threw a tantrum. The servants *had* to lift the pot and put it down outside the house. Paurav then caressed the leaves of the plant and said, "You bathe in the sunshine, while I go to Chocolate Uncle's house. Okay?"

Two days earlier, Paurav had fallen down from a mango tree while trying to pluck some raw fruit. He had fallen into a heap of dry leaves. The gardener, who was standing below the tree, had immediately lifted up Paurav and made sure that he was not seriously hurt. Earlier, the gardener had complained to the master about Paurav's climbing trees once too often. The father had put the matter aside, and had continued to read his paper. But now, hearing Paurav's mad talk of the plant walking and talking, he got worried: had Paurav injured his brain in the fall from the tree? Mithubhai was a well-known neurologist, and a friend. Paurav was always ready to go to his house because Mithubhai gave him chocolates; and so Paurav's pet name for him was Chocolate Uncle.

Paurav was carefully examined from all angles. Mithubhai opined that there was no injury to Paurav's brain. Dr. Mehta's mind was plagued by questions. Paurav would never lie, since truthfulness had been ingrained in the children. The parents had raised Paurav and his elder sister Paulomi with loving care and without using threats of punishment. Either the plant's walking and talking was a delusion, or he was incapable of sharing Paurav's experience. What was the truth? Dr. Mehta kept pondering the whole day.

In time the matter got buried like a relic of the past. Since Dr. Mehta relished the society of plants, he and his family lived in a garden house some fifteen kilometers from the city of Ahmedabad. Like multi-hued clouds, chiku, custard apple, rayan, berry, jamun, mango, coconut and date palms, along with the flowering trees of gulmohur, acacia, bohemia, and so forth graced the sky of Dr. Mehta's garden. He had planted a variety of trees, some brought from abroad, that were suited to the water and soil of the garden. There was a greenhouse adjacent to the house, in which, for the past two years, Dr. Mehta had been raising several African plants.

The father had been teaching botany to Paurav and Paulomi from early childhood. The five-year old Paurav already knew well the names of the plants growing in the garden, and the names of their flowers, fruits and seed. He also knew well the seasons in which the plants flowered and fruited. He could easily empathize with plants and trees. Sunday mornings were devoted to experiments and fun with numbers. The father would get Paulomi to conduct simple experiments on things of daily usage. Paurav ran about helping in gathering the materials. He would intently watch the experiments, but still he was too small to understand much.

Rupande, the mother, was raised in an orthodox Vaishnava[1*] family. She thought of her two children as incarnations of infant Krishna. She had an inexhaustible store of wondrous tales. Every night the children would refuse to go to bed until they heard a story from Ramayana or Mahabharata, or an episode from the lives of 84 Vaishnavas, or from biographies of saints. She took a lot of interest in the children's education, though she herself had not gone to college.

Today Paurav is celebrating his seventh birthday. Mother has made jalebi—a great favourite of Paurav. It is the beginning of July. The school is closed because of heavy rains. From the morning Paurav is busy transferring small plants from pots to the earth. He is whistling and breaking the pots and transplanting, taking care not to tear their roots. But one pot slips from his hands and shatters as it falls to the ground. The soil inside scatters and the small roots break. Paurav screams.

Rupande and Paulomi come running and see Paurav holding the plant in his hands and sobbing. Wiping his tears, the mother asks affectionately:
"What happened Paurav?"
"Ma! This little plant fell from my hands . . ." Paurav is frightened, and starts crying as if he is hurt.

Paulomi curls her index finger near her temple to signal to the mother that the brother has gone crazy. The mother is shaken—what is this madness that has afflicted her son!

For a while Paurav keeps caressing the plant without saying a word. Then he digs a small hole in the ground, plants it, and waters it with a pipe.

"Look, Ma! He seems less afraid now, doesn't he? Look! Now isn't he more erect?"

The mother takes his fingers and leads him away towards the kitchen.

1 followers of Lord Vishnu

Paurav went frequently to examine the plant, like a doctor keeping a careful eye on a patient. The next night he was very chirpy at the dining table. He talked proudly of how he tended the plant and how the plant had become his intimate friend. Paulomi could not control her mirth, and she burst out laughing—like a spray of colour from a spout at Holi[2*]. Rupande thought her son had really lost his mind. The dinner over, the plates removed, the mother and daughter left; but the father and son kept sitting at the table engrossed in botanical talk.

With the passage of years, Paurav's circle of botanical friends grew large. Paurav created a small vegetable garden. Ten-year old Paurav had the skills of a seasoned gardener. At the winter's onset he had asked his father to get the seeds of cabbage, carrot, tomato, cauliflower, etc. He raked the soil with the help of the gardener, mingled manure in it, and sowed high quality seed. In a month many a vegetable head pierced the earth. Every head was Paurav's kin, and like a mother moving around storing the faces of all her children in her heart, Paurav intimately knew every head of vegetable in the garden. He would get up early in the morning and go off to see his red-green-orange-white infants, ask them how they were doing and chat with them, not with his tongue though, but telepathically.

One of his cabbages had got shriveled. All the other cabbages had fat, round faces; but this miss grew neither during the day nor the night! Every morning Paurav mentally asked her: "Cabbage, tell me what's on your mind, what's troubling you?" Once the cabbage transmitted a message: "O brother, worms are stuck to my roots, nibbling away day and night, sucking out all my juices. And that is why my body is wasting away."

Paurav dug out some of the surrounding soil, put some insecticide around the cabbage, and sprayed the cabbage's body, too, with it. In a few days the cabbage began to fatten, and lustrous green began to shimmer on its surface.

2 A spring festival during which people spray colours on each other

Initially, since Paurav and the vegetables conversed telepathically, Paurav wondered whether a message was from one of them or he mistook his own thoughts for those of the vegetable! As soon as Paurav arrived at the vegetable garden, he would find all the vegetables in glee, like pups wagging their tails. He would stroke as many of them as he could, and their love would infuse his mind. Feeding on Paurav's love, water and manure, all the vegetables had become fresh and succulent. Whenever a vegetable felt that it was ripe, it communicated to Paurav to harvest it. Every day Paurav used to bring to the kitchen a small basket filled with vegetables.

One day the vegetables in the kitchen were exhausted. Rupande was unwell and so she could not go to the market. She asked the cook to fetch cabbages from Paurav's garden. The cook took a knife and quickly harvested several.

Paurav was in school, working on sums given by the teacher. Suddenly he heard the cries of his beloved friends: "Save us! Save us!" He keenly felt their agony. Paurav could not do the sums. The arithmetic class was the day's last class and the school bell rang as soon as it got over. Paurav ran and sat in his car at the school's gate. Paulomi had not arrived yet. Paulomi would always get into the car as soon as the school got over, and Paurav, joking and talking with his friends, would get to the car 15-20 minutes late. Paulomi would daily get annoyed with Paurav.

That day, though, Paurav was so keen to get to his garden and see how his friends were doing, that like a hurricane he ran to Paulomi's class. He seized her hand and ran dragging her to the car. The panting Paulomi kept peering at him in astonishment and anger. Then, in a voice raised to the rooftops she berated him: "You daily keep me waiting in the car. Then are you bothered about time? Now I will also drag you to the car this way."

The car started moving. Paurav sat in silence. Paulomi could not understand why the perpetual radio was silent. She asked many questions, but they merely collided with his pre-occupied mind and returned. As soon as they got home, Paurav practically jumped out of the still moving car and ran to his garden. Paurav felt the way we would, if we were to walk on the Kurukshetra battlefield, and our stomach would churn as we viewed innumerable corpses smeared with blood. How many of his friends had been massacred! Remembering their faces, Paurav sat there, waves of anguish crashing incessantly on his face. He was most pained at the fate of his favourite, the barely ripened cabbage. "Why did you leave me? How lonely I will feel without you?" He wailed mentally. So sharp was his pain that stunned time stood still.

Mother came to the garden looking for Paurav. Paurav's eyes overflowed with tears at seeing his mother, as he sought refuge in her love and consolation. The mother sat by Paurav, caressing his head, and began to cry herself.
"Son! Will you forgive me?"
"Ma! You cut . . . !"
"Son! How could I know that you see them as human?"
"Ma! You are a killer."

The word 'killer' pierced the mother's heart and the pain tumbled forth in sobs. Neither could see the other's face, since their eyes were filled with tears. Like blind persons sensing their surroundings through ears, their ears kept reacting to their agonised sobbing.

The father arrived at the scene. Paulomi had provided the background. He caught hold of Paurav's arm and gently steered him along as he walked towards home. The mother got up and trailed behind them. Paurav ran to his room and shut the door from inside. The dinner bell rang three times that day, but his door remained shut.

For a few days, speech was muted at home. When the home again turned chirpy, the father talked at length with his son.
"Paurav! Do you converse with plants through your lips? Like you do with me?"
"No."
"Do the messages from plants come to your mind as thoughts, or as pictures?"

"I keep on seeing pictures, as if one is viewing the pictures of an Amar Charit Katha picture-story. But the pictures are quite different. They are far more alive."
"But can the pictures you see in your mind not be your imagination?"
"Pappa! I can't explain this; but I do converse with plants, and as distinctly as my present conversation with you is."
"But can this be true just because you say so?"
"Pappa! You mean I am lying?"
"No son! Your experience is certainly real—and this natural gift of yours must be developed. How wonderful it is! But it would be great if you can prove it scientifically. Because then the way would be opened for people like me who want to communicate with plants."
"Pappa! I am still so young!"
"But you will certainly grow up! My heart says you will make some major discovery in botany."

Paurav hugged his father.

Five years have passed. How tall Paurav has grown during this time, first inching above his mother's shoulders, and then head! He is still slightly shorter than his father, but you can notice this only if the father and the son stand side-by-side. He has completely forgotten whining, and indeed, he is ashamed of crying. Childish prattle has gone for ever, and in the throat a voice has ripened—so like his father's! On the phone Rupande sometimes mistakes the son for the father! Growing up has opened many petals of understanding. Even Paurav does not know how and when the fingers of his parents slipped out of his hands. Now he puts his hands around his father's shoulders and gives his mother the support of his strong shoulders.

Paurav is dreaming of becoming a botanist like his father. He is still as interested in the life of plants as he was earlier; but his love for it has been suppressed somewhat by the abundant fruiting of his intelligence. That love does sometimes try to raise its head, but logic keeps it down under its steely paws.

Paurav was in deep slumber. Suddenly he sensed that the gulmohur tree growing adjacent to his window was telling him to get up at once. He had planted the sapling with his own hands years earlier. Paurav got up with a start, and looked out of the window at the gulmohur. It was dancing with its innumerable big and small fronds. The bulky branches swaying in the breeze swung back and forth in his mind. He touched, within his being, the tiny, trellised, fresh green leaves, slippery like a squirrel's tail. All its twigs turned tender, like his mother's fingers. He felt as if he was bodily lifted by the fingers of the gulmohur—like the way his mother's hand steered him when he was small. The gulmohur's fingers nudged him down the stairs, and made him stand in the kitchen. Paurav felt perplexed, seeking a rational explanation. But now he vividly felt being part of the weave of the silken, lace-like branches of the gulmohur, and under its silken control. The affection, suppressed during recent years, suddenly, swiftly bloomed!

Just then, outside the kitchen door, which looked out into the garden, there was the sound of a vessel falling. Speech, so far stuck to the palate, now broke free and a shout of "Who is there?" burst out of Paurav's throat. In response, feet scurried away. Paurav switched on the light. He shouted for his father. The father rushed pell-mell to the kitchen.
"Pappa! There was a sound of a vessel falling outside this door—then some one ran."
"Stay put. I will get a torch."
The father got the torch and tried to open the door—but the door was open! Outside sprawled an open bundle, containing vessels. Next to it was a long knife. However, it belonged to the house.
"When did you come down?"
"Just a minute before I shouted to you."
"Why did you come down?"
"Pappa! The gulmohur outside my window made me come down." Barely hearing the words, the father called the police. A police team came and noted down in detail the attempted theft.

After this event, for some days there was incessant chewing on many questions: who broke in; how; for what purpose; what other things besides vessels could have been stolen had Paurav been late. Paurav hardly participated in all this discussion. Instead, a single question occupied Paurav's mind: "Why did the gulmohur wake me? It must have feelings for me. Why for me, and not for Pappa? May be there is feeling for Pappa also, but he is not able to experience it."

Paurav's memory slid to age five. He saw his little hands digging a small pit in the ground, putting some manure in it. A couple of years later, straddling a wall, he was caressing the feathery leaves of the gulmohur. After this event two Pauravs started living together in the same house—one was five years old; the other, sixteen.

On entering college, Paurav chose botany, since he wanted to get a deep understanding of plant behaviour. He also wanted to prove scientifically that humans have a psychic bond with plants.

Even our ancestors strongly believed that there is life in vegetation. They also believed that plants experience pleasure and pain, and so considered it a sin to cut any vegetation after sunset. They thought that like humans, plants also close their eyelids and sleep at night. Paurav often wondered how primitive man thought before language was created. Paurav tried to think without words; but he could not quite fathom a non-verbal thought process.

He started creating an apparatus in his laboratory. It had a plastic dial. At the centre was a red circle. Outside it was a blue circle, and outside this, a golden circle. It could be hung on any tree or plant. If the plant was delighted, the golden circle lit up. If it experienced pain, the inner red circle lit up, and if it was calm like the waters of a lake, then the middle blue circle lit up.

Paurav conducted many experiments. He would put predatory worms among the roots of a plant; soon the middle red circle would light up. If leaves were torn or a tree trunk scratched, then the red circle would light up only for a second or two. The blue circle would always light up after sunset. In the cool breeze of the morning, when the leaves still dozed, bathing in the fountain of sunshine, the golden circle would light up. But in the afternoon, the golden circle was very faint. The intensity of illumination varied directly with the intensity of the plant's experience.

After many experiments, Paurav exhibited his dial in his college's science exhibition. The professors and students of the college went gaga over

Paurav's invention. The principal patted Paurav on his back and said, "You are the pride of our college." Paurav's father was present at the inauguration of the exhibition. On viewing his son's discovery, he inflated like a balloon and soared high with pride and pleasure. Till that day Paurav had kept his discovery a secret. Dr. Mehta had studied all his life the biological being of plants; but he had never thought of their subtle psychic processes. His face shone at the son outshining him. Those present kept looking at Paurav's dad; everyone was wondering perhaps about the kind of magical upbringing that was responsible for such an achievement.

Rupande could not go to the exhibition because of guests at home. Besides, how would she know that her son was going to be the centre of attention at the exhibition? On returning home, the husband verbally painted in vivid colours the scene of the exhibition. Her eyes first turned moist; then tears began to flow. Ecstatic, Paulomi thumped Paurav's back three-four times; then hugged him hard.

Like the sages of old, Paurav practices penance for years—to discover, despite pain, a demonstrable, scientific mode of conversing with vegetation.

In an open field, standing in a circle, twenty-five men are screaming at a tall coconut tree. About fifty others are sitting around them. As soon as the screamers tire, they are replaced by those in the outer circle. This goes on for all twenty-four hours of the day. Dr. Mehta and Paulomi are carefully supervising the whole experiment. Paurav is nowhere to be seen; he has left the experiment to his father and sister because he cannot bear the agony the tree feels because of the terrifying screams.

No effect on the tree is visible for the first two days. On the third day the fronds of the tree begin to droop. In six days, they wither. As the roots turn weaker, the tree begins to list a little. The screamers hired by Paurav for the experiment get excited when they find the tree bending. On the eighth day, the tree falls. Those participating in the experiment shout a big hurrah.

When Paurav learns of the tree's fall, he feels like a murderer. He keeps stealing away from his own eyes.

Next day, the newspapers feature, on the front page, the photo of Paurav embracing the healthy coconut tree before the experiment. Next to it is the photo of the fallen tree on day eight. Below the photos are the details of the experiment. The last line is his quote: "I did this experiment to convince rationalists; but otherwise the response of plants to human emotions is my daily experience."

For many days people flock to behold the dead coconut tree. Their eyes long to see the creator of the experiment. But who can imagine that he is in deep mourning at the tree's demise?

Paurav firmly believed that trees have a special consciousness, and that is why we feel so peaceful sitting under them. Whenever Paurav felt ill he would go and hide like a bird in a tree's foliage. It was as if the tree absorbed Paurav's sickness. When the father of a friend of Paurav heard this from Paurav, he laughed in derision.

Paurav said: "Uncle! Instead of laughing this away, why don't you test this out with an experiment? Can we get fifteen of your patients suffering from a chronic illness to sit under a tree's foliage for three hours a day?"
"Under which tree's foliage?"

"The banyan tree opposite your house would be ideal."

The doctor was not much interested, for he had no faith in this experiment. But Paurav pressed him hard with Hanuman[3] tenacity, and the experiment began.

3 a devotee of Rama, who developed enormous tenacity and strength through devotion

A motley crowd of patients has been assembled: four are heart patients, three have skin problems, two are epileptic, and so on. The way the doctor provides the background for the experiment, no one but a fool would like to participate in it. But Paurav inspires them to participate with his experience-infused, authentic words.

Daily, from 4.30 p.m. to 7.30 p.m. fifteen patients sit and sleep in the banyan's shade, silently praying to the tree to cure them. Paurav makes one thing very clear: "Do not participate in the experiment if you doubt the tree's consciousness."

In fifteen days most of the patients feel a notable improvement. A few find no change; but all experience mental peace. There is commotion in the world of doctors.

There is a reference in India's ancient scriptures that trees are former sages. When Paurav read this he felt that there was a deep meaning in this.

One day, Paurav was sitting on a cot under a pipal tree, watching its leaves chattering and laughing in the wind. He felt its exuberance. His mind started roaming:

> *The tree is vast—its head is up in the sky and its roots seek stability by spreading underground, even if this requires piercing rocks. Maybe the tree, because of its height, catches some special waves in the atmosphere that humans can't? Trees were meditating on their earthly asanas many ages before man's advent on the earth. The tree cannot walk; nor can it use its branches as limbs for its defense; nor can it squash anyone under its elephantine bulk. The tree practices the supreme form of non-violence. Could it be that the tree is spiritually far more advanced than man? Besides, it is self-sufficient in food. It draws whatever food and water it needs from the bowels of the earth, and from sunlight. If humans could learn from trees how to harness solar energy for their nourishment, then hunger could be banished from the world.*

Stepping back in time, Paurav is now a child. He remembers the tales his mother had told him of Krishna's sports. As a punishment, Yashoda, the mother, ties mischievous little Krishna to a mortar. Dragging the mortar, Krishna emerges from between two adjacent trees. The trees are uprooted, and two divine beings, both gatekeepers of Lord Vishnu, emerge from them.

Little Paurav is borne along by the current of the story. He stares at the trees and rubs himself against one of them, so that any divine being hidden in it would manifest itself!

Weaving a garland of thoughts, his eyes begin to perceive the fantastic, as if a tree has touched his eyelids with its magic finger. Sitting down in a meditative posture under a peepal tree, with his hands in a gesture of supplication, Paurav prays to the tree to make him one.

"You want to be a tree? Why?" The peepal asks, swaying overhead in the breeze.
"I want to become tall and touch the sky with my head."
"If someone wants to cut off your feet, you will not be able to stop him."
"If I can have your endurance, I don't mind my feet being cut."
"This wondrous power is of green blood. But in you flows the red blood of rage!"
"That blood I will spill on the ground. Will you then pour your sap into me?"

Paurav watches red blood drip to the ground from his big toe. The green of the peepal tree begins to enter into his body, and rises to his eyes. His entire body is suffused with verdant waves.

Paurav awakens from his reverie; but there is a green shimmer in his eyes. Paurav is human; but now also tree!

PETER

Years ago I used to teach in a college in Montreal. Montreal is in Canada's Quebec province. Quebec has mostly French-speaking but also some English-speaking people. The stamp of these two mighty cultures clearly shows on the city's architecture, clothing, literature, music, and cuisine. The fusion of these two cultures is like the blending of fine spices in a gourmet meal.

The year I started teaching in this college I got to know an Indian student. That friendship is still just as fresh. I have so far taught countless students; but this one was special. When I took attendance, some students would call out "Present" and some others would say "Yes, ma'am"; but this boy would say: "I am"! When his turn came I would raise my head from the register and look at him, and he would look into my eyes and say with aplomb, "I am."

After six or seven classes I called him and asked, "Peter, why do you say 'I am' while marking presence?"

With mischief flashing in his eyes, Peter said, "I have no doubt about my existence. But even I do not know whether I am present in the class or not because my mind keeps vaulting. And saying 'madam-fadam' just does not suit my style."

He laughed sweetly like a rasagolla[4]. There were beguiling dimples in his cheeks and chin. The contours of his face altered. The cheeks were raised, the eyes became slits, the lips were lengthened in parting, the teeth shone

---

4 sweetened, spongy cheese balls

and a golden-pink hue covered his face. I felt a wave of affection for him rise within me but forced it to subside because our acquaintance was not yet deep. He waved his arms and head and said: "Okay?" Then he ran off from the class.

The subject of my course was 'Quest of the Self', that is, the uncovering of the dimensions of one's self. We are not aware of many facets of our selves. Others around us often observe and analyze our personality in minute detail. If people close to us tell us frankly how we appear to them, then our false beliefs about ourselves and our blind spots could get corrected. In my class we helped each other to try to find out more about our true selves.

One day we played an interesting game about how we view our own appearance. Each student held a mirror in turn and opined on his or her facial appearance. I asked laughingly, "Who will start off?" Every student sat with averted eyes lest our gaze met and I asked the person to start. For a few moments there was the deep silence of space. I broke it by asking the girl sitting to my left to start. One by one the students took the mirror and spoke about their faces. Many berated their face with gusto, perhaps because they felt too embarrassed to praise it. Some were not comfortable looking at their face!

Peter was the last. Only that day I had come to know that his real name was Padmanabh. He had anglicized it to Peter, because Canadians found it difficult to pronounce such a tongue-twister. Peter took the mirror in style. First he contracted his features as if he was lost in thought. He said, "I look different in different situations. When I am in deep thought my eyes retreat a bit in their sockets and my cheeks flatten out like a flattened cardboard box. My nose turns into a hook for hanging clothes. I look clever because of my knitted eyebrows."

Then he changed his expression. Looking into the mirror, he started laughing loudly: "I look very attractive when I laugh. My whole face blooms like a garden." Then he made his face weepy. "Now my entire face looks like a landslide. Anyone seeing me now would feel as if he has just taken a laxative." The entire class broke into laughter. Like a physician in a mobile chair examining a patient from different angles, his mind could take in a thing or a situation from many angles.

This is Peter's third and last year in college. There are daily debates at home on what he should do next. Peter has no interest in any long-lettered degree. And it is against his nature to do what others do. His parents are intent on his becoming a doctor. In North America doctors earn a lot; besides, a doctor at home would be a great help in old age!

Peter's father, Mr. Gupta, is a computer science expert. Mother Danielle, a French-Canadian, is a fine musician. Peter has no kinship, direct or indirect, with music. He also firmly believes that it is lot more fun interacting with people than with a computer, so there is not much possibility of his taking that line. From childhood his gullet was never wide enough to swallow anyone's advice! From the beginning his parents had so strongly encouraged him to question everything that now they regret his not being under their thumb.

Some days earlier Peter had got hold of the biography of Ramakrishna Paramhamsa, the 19th century Indian divine. While scanning a library shelf, his eyes lit upon the book. Opening it, Peter saw the photograph of Ramakrishna. He was standing with a hand raised in a wondrous gesture of ecstasy. Peter wanted to know more about his life. For a whole week Peter was intoxicated with Ramakrishna.

One day, when I got to my office, Peter was lounging outside the door with his feet outstretched. He got up when he saw me. He put the book on Ramakrishna in my hand and said: "Ramakrishna has changed my entire being."
"What appealed most to you in Ramakrishna's life?"
"He was like a scientist who tests a hypothesis with many experiments. What a mighty soul! He proved the existence of God through spiritual experiments! He proved this by following each religion in turn and by realizing God through each!"
"I am also totally fascinated by Ramakrishna."
"Have you been to Dakshineshwar?"[5]

5 The place outside Kolkata where Ramakrishna lived.

"Many times."
He grabbed my hand and sat in the chair next to mine. We discussed Ramakrishna for hours.
"Who were the other great souls of Ramakrishna's stature in India during the 20th century?"
I gave the names of Ramana Maharshi and Gandhiji. Peter began the study of both. He would run to me whenever he got confused. Within a month he had browsed through several books.

Then he felt a strong urge to go to India and get acquainted with its saints and great souls. After thinking about this for several days he announced his decision to his parents.

"I am not yet ready to choose any particular direction for my life. I still need many experiences. I want to go to India and meet saints, yogis, and ascetics."
"What is the point of meeting them?" The father asked.
"Perhaps meeting them will make me grow in a way neither you nor I can anticipate."

The parents thought that this fad born of reading books would soon wane. That summer Peter worked in a bookshop to earn money for his trip.

The parents got a fright when one day Peter came home with an air ticket for India. The flight was on June 4th. Peter was really going! Despite his parents' disapproval, Peter declared that his decision was final. They felt that it was a blunder to raise him and let him develop his personality in unbridled freedom. Had they kept him on leash they could have ordered him to stay.

Peter decided to go first to Delhi and then to Badrinath because he had heard or read about the miracle in the temple there. Though there is no one in the temple during the four months of winter, the lamp inside keeps burning, and fresh flowers get offered daily to the idol of Lord Badrinath. He would believe this only if he saw with his own eyes; he would not accept a mere legend.

When the parents went to the airport to see their son off, they felt helpless—like watching the water in one's fist trickle away. The moment of parting came. Peter embraced his mother and father. Tears flickered in the eyes of all three. His parents' gazes followed him until he disappeared behind the security check portal. Then they turned back with vacant eyes.

As soon as Peter settled into his seat the air hostess began her spiel: "Fasten your seat belts . . . in the unlikely event of the cabin pressure falling, an oxygen mask will automatically descend . . .". Peter resumed reading Gandhiji's 'My Experiments with Truth'. How did this mighty soul walk; eat? How would his external behaviour be different from that of the common man? Thus ruminating, Peter fell asleep. Finally Delhi came.

Mr. Ashish Bannerji, a close friend of Peter's father, had come to receive Peter. Mr. Bannerji and Peter's father had earlier been colleagues in IBM's office in Montreal. For the last six years Mr. Bannerji was the manager of IBM's Delhi office. The moment you enter Mr. Bannerji's house you would think you are in a Canadian home. Every article in the house has been brought from Canada. Coughing and fingering his diamond ring, Mr. Bannerji kept recounting the prices of all the articles he was proud of and the names of the Canadian stores he had bought them from. Fed up with this unending litany, Peter asked, "Uncle, do you have any old Indian art pieces?"
"Is anything worthwhile available in this country?" Bannerji wrinkled his nose in disdain. "Anyone wanting to be in hell should come here. It is no sign of intelligence to waste one's time in this dung heap!"
"You were born in this country by mistake, isn't it uncle?"

The doorbell rang. Peter opened the door. Carrying a mountain of books in her arms, Mr. Bannerji's daughter Saloni came into the room. The eyes of both opened wide as they stared at each other. "Uncle! Saloni has grown in so many ways in six years! Both vertically and horizontally! Had I met her on the road I would not have recognized her. But then I would certainly have tried to get to know her", Peter said, winking. Saloni cast her eyes down in modesty. Six years earlier in Montreal, Saloni was ten and Peter was fifteen. Then Peter was barely sprouting a moustache; but

Saloni was just a bud opening its petals. Peter remembered Saloni clearly because he was older, but Saloni's memory of him was hazy. In just a few hours their friendship became fresh again, and in a week they became such close friends that Peter wanted to take Saloni with him to Badrinath!

At 4.45 in the morning Peter is settled in his seat in the 5 o'clock bus to Hardwar, located on River Ganga. Peter is carrying only a haversack. Over Peter's vigorous protest, both Mr. Bannerji and Saloni have come to the bus stand to see him off. Saloni is quietly standing beneath Peter's window. Mr. Bannerji is standing in the bus near Peter and ticking off his list of advices. But they merely collide with Peter's inattentive ears, not enter them. Peter's attention is on Saloni, who is standing beneath his window. The bus starts. Saloni and Peter keep on waving their hands like flags, until they turn into dots.

Black and blue after a bumpy ride, Peter was quite drained out by the time Hardwar came. So he took a taxi to Rishikesh, further upstream. That night he slept soundly in Maharshi Mahesh's posh ashram. By morning he was fresh. He was keen on tracking on foot from Rishikesh to Badrinath, and set out to look for a reliable guide. Since Peter was on the fair side and looked like a foreigner, people crowded around him like ants round a sweetmeat. Just then, an ordinary looking man elbowed aside the people surrounding Peter. He advanced to the centre of the crowd, and casually asked, "You don't have any problems, do you?"
"No—I want to go to Badrinath on foot. Can somebody accompany me?" Peter answered in his broken Hindi.
"What is there in Badrinath? Even buses go there. But Jamnotri is worth seeing. That's the source of our holy river Jamna. Come with me if you like. The road is really wild—but enchanting."

His name was Shridhar. Peter was surprised, and a bit suspicious about this invitation from a total stranger. But there was a look of purity in Shridhar 's eyes, and his suspicion subsided.

"What is so special about Jamnotri?"
"An exalted one who is my guru lives there in a cave. You will have the good fortune of having his 'darshan.'[6] For the last four or five days he

6 auspicious sight

has been intimating to me telepathically that a person will meet me in Rishikesh and that I should bring him over to him." Peter stared at Shridhar in some alarm.

Shridhar took Peter's hand as if they were old friends and led him to a nearby tea stall. Both sat down on a bench, and while sipping tea, Shridhar told his story.

Many years back Shridhar was going to Jamnotri on a pilgrimage. On the way, suddenly his feet got rooted to the ground. For several minutes he stood glued to the ground, helpless and uneasy.

As if sawed through by a blade made of lightning, a big ledge broke some distance above him and crashed down. Had he been walking, he would certainly have been crushed by the landslide. Shridhar was convinced that some power had saved him. He heard footsteps behind him. When he looked back he saw a sadhu[7] in a loincloth and with a great 'jata'[8] coming towards him. He was laughing. His eyes were radiant like the noon sun. This man had a god-like body. He was tall and strongly built, and his finely etched face swayed a little like a branch laden with blossoms. He had long, wavy, silvery hair, and a silver beard descended like a waterfall from his mouth. Shridhar 's feet came unstuck at the approach of this divine person, and he prostrated at his feet. Shridhar entered his cave, pulled along as if by an invisible string. Shridhar stayed on for three-four months in the sage's fragrant company.

Peter felt a strong urge to meet this sage and he decided to go along with Shridhar. Rising impatiently, Peter said, "Can we get started? Daylight will soon wane. Let us talk on the way."

To Peter this unexpected meeting with Shridhar seemed a miracle. Who would they meet on the way? What would Shridhar 's guru say when he saw him? Would the guru have the effulgence and the power that Shridhar described? Such questions kept surfacing in Peter's mind in step with his tramping feet.

---

7 seeker of truth

8 bun of hair on the head

Peter gets high on a panorama where beauty itself has become wonder-struck. On and on they walk, and rest only when they are exhausted. Before sunset they pitch their tent for the night. Peter has hired a man for the journey. This man loads all the baggage on his pony. In the evening he pitches the tent, cooks hot food and feeds them. The prior night's story continues in the lamp's light.

From childhood Shridhar had deep faith in God. He was born in a very poor family and he was the last of six children. The parents were all the time tense from the burden of feeding their brood. There was a daily dessert of thrashings for the children. The huts encroached on each other, like trees in a dense jungle. There was no feel there of light or air. Thousands of naked, helpless children with running nose, whose future was interred before their birth, buzzed around like flies.

Shridhar stood apart from his siblings. He had neither friend nor foe. He spent all day reciting the Lord's name. His parents and siblings thought he was a fool. There was a small garden near the slum. He used to sit on a bench, watch the trees in the garden, and sing with deep feeling devotional songs in a rich baritone. Adjacent to the garden was a factory manufacturing metal sheets. The owner of this factory was religious and loved devotional songs. Once, during a night shift, the owner came to the garden and sat on a bench to enjoy the cool breeze. Shridhar was singing with fervour. The owner was deeply moved. He approached Shridhar and asked him questions. He came to know of Shridhar's situation. He gave Shridhar a job in his factory. He was to keep the factory clean, and sing devotional songs whenever the owner wished to hear them. Shridhar firmly believed that God was bearing all his burdens—and so he felt light as a feather. After meeting his guru, Shridhar went unfailingly every year to Jamnotri for his 'darshan'. He felt he was the happiest of men.

Shridhar opens his life to Peter; but shows no desire to learn anything about Peter. Peter feels that at this stage it is best to remain quiet, and so he discloses very little about himself. On the third day Shirdhar brings Peter to his guru's dwelling. The sage is sitting on a deerskin outside a cave, with his eyes closed. On opening his eyes, he shows no surprise at Shridhar and Peter sitting there. First Shirdhar, and then, imitating Shridhar, Peter, prostrate before him. He seems to have known Peter, and has been expecting him. Peter experiences in his presence an alien peace never experienced before. The sage seldom speaks, and the two friends also do not feel like marring the serenity with words. There is communication here, but mostly in silence. In the morning the two friends go out to gather fruits and flowers, and then they talk to their hearts' content. The sage neither asks their name and address nor speaks to them about himself. He seems totally fearless. Otherwise how can one live the year round in this cave dense with darkness?

Peter was frightened of the dark from his childhood and so at sunset he confined himself to the cave, content with the dim light of a lamp. One night the sage roused Peter from his sleep and asked him to accompany him. Peter was shivering inside; but he obeyed. The sage was totally fearless and Peter felt shielded by his power. After walking for two-three miles on a narrow path they came to a valley. Nearby, a waterfall thundered. The sage sat on a large rock and he asked Peter to sit on one opposite his. For the past several days Peter had been turning over some questions in his mind, and he mustered up courage to ask them now:

"Why do I feel peace in your presence?"
"I am tranquil and you are in my lap."
"Are peace and God separate?"
"The universe within us, and we in the universe—through this ceaseless experience of mutual immanence we perceive God. Whoever has had this experience is totally at peace."
"Why don't you have any fear?"
"If I pervade everything, how can I be afraid!"
"But . . ."
"This is not a matter for logic. Let it pass now. We will talk about this telepathically after twenty years. All your questions will vanish in the light of experience."

The sage asked Peter to come and sit by him. The sage put his hand on Peter's head. Peter began to see a tossing, swaying ocean of light. After a while he felt himself taking the form of that light. He became the light, and mingled with this ocean. For hours Peter remained lost in this state. When Peter opened his eyes he felt the jolt of being cast from a celestial universe to a nether universe.

By now the fingers of the sun were stirring up everything within their reach. Beside this enormous experience Peter felt that all his past experiences were puny. When the two reached the cave they found Shridhar sitting near its entrance. Later, when Shridhar and Peter went to gather flowers and fruits, Peter narrated the entire episode of the night. The sage had given Shridhar a taste of this experience years back. Thereafter only had Shridhar accepted the sage as his guru.

Days kept slipping away. The two friends kept hoarding all the treasure they could contain within them. With his spiritual power, the sage had given Peter a peak experience; but this tide began to ebb and Peter's mind began to thirst for leaving this serenity and returning to the city's hubbub. As if divining this, the sage told the two friends to go home. The next day they took the blessings of the sage and left Jamnotri.

They reached Hardwar. From there the two friends were to diverge. Peter had to go to Bannerji's house in Delhi and Shridhar had to leave for his slum in Mumbai. However, Shridhar could persuade Peter to travel to Mumbai and stay with him for a few days. Peter wrote to Mr. Bannerji that he would return to Delhi after spending a few days in Mumbai. Both got into the train for Mumbai. Peter, brought up in Canadian affluence, wanted to experience the piercing poverty of a slum. He had frequently seen slums on Canadian television. But Peter wanted to be an inmate in a slum and measure his tolerance capacity. How long would the tranquility bestowed by the sage last in a slum, Peter mused, and smiled to himself at the thought.

On the way to Mumbai Peter gave his complete life-sketch to Shridhar, but told him to keep this secret. Shridhar felt a deep respect for Peter. They got off at Bombay Central station and took a local train to Bandra. They felt hemmed in, in the overcrowded compartment. After getting off at Bandra they began to walk towards Shridhar 's slum. Along the way Peter bought gifts for every member of Shridhar's family.

When the two friends entered Shridhar's hut, one of the sisters was darning a torn sari with her feet spread wide. A second sister was squatting on a cot like a monkey, taking lice out of the hair of a third sister. The mother was busy in a corner cooking rice and daal. The men folk were absent. The father had gone off with his handcart to collect old household things for trade. Two brothers, sharp-eyed like falcons, one fourteen and the other fifteen, were busy picking up butts of cigarettes from the road. They made bundles of the longer butts for sale in the slum and thereby earned money for their clothes and two-three movies a week. The three sisters winked at one another and smiled slyly on seeing a stranger enter the hut. Shridhar took Peter inside and introduced him to his mother. He told her that he was going to stay with them for a few days. Peter greeted her courteously. The mother greeted Peter, but with a grimace. Peter was repelled by this roughness, but consoled himself that silken courtesy can last only in affluence. He was amazed that Shridhar had survived in this slime without getting sullied.

The behaviour of the sisters and the mother changed as soon as Peter took out some blouse-pieces and auspicious vermilion from Hardwar. The four compared the tint and pattern of their cloth pieces. Then one of them ran to get Peter a glass of water and two sisters spread a mat for him. The mother said, "Good of you to come." Shridhar was not there when the men-folk returned for the afternoon meal. The sisters and the mother introduced Peter to the men folk and noisily broadcast the details of Peter's presents.

It did not take long for chatty Peter to get to know the local people. In four or five days, Peter came to know of the many peculiarities of the slum. He got familiar with the language used in their quarrels, reasons for the quarrels, the black trades going on there, the peculiar diseases rampant there, the rites of marriage, the disdain for education, the hero-worship of film stars, the poor quality of diet, the stinking filth.

In the whole slum there were just two taps, and water came only once, at six in the evening. A train-long queue would form for water—not just of humans but also of buckets and other containers. Tongues would clash should anybody push someone else's vessel back in the queue. Choicest abuses would flow and arms would flail about like batons. Everyday Peter would join the queue to get ten to fifteen buckets of water for Shridhar's hut. He would entertain others with interesting tales while waiting to fill water, and act as referee to settle quarrels. Shridhar would go to the factory at nine and Peter would then enter one of the huts. Sometimes he would tell stories to children; sometimes he would talk to the women and help them in their work. He would talk to the aged about religious matters of their interest, and would willingly volunteer to perform some of their chores.

Thus, in a few days a lot of people have come to know Peter. They have been charmed by his way of talking, walking, his fair complexion, and his smooth, cascading hair—in short by his very attractive persona.

Peter often went to Shridhar's factory in the evening. Practically every day he met Shridhar's employer and discussed many topics with him. From Peter's talk and conduct Shridhar's employer realized that Peter was not the scion of an ordinary family. Peter got the idea of starting a small night school for the slum's youth. He requested Shridhar 's employer to spare a room in his factory for the school.

When he was young, this factory owner had often thought of contributing to the welfare of slums, but he had not been able to overcome his family's fierce opposition to this. He agreed with pleasure to Peter's proposal, and provided all help. The school began in a fortnight. Youngsters of 12 to 16 years of age gathered there at 8.30 at night.

On the first day Peter asked each youngster: "What do you wish to be, and why?" Practically everybody wanted to become wealthy so as 'to enjoy life'. Peter had earlier met a number of persons living around the slum and had discussed in detail with them the kinds of work these youngsters could be trained to do to make a decent living. Peter had been strongly influenced by Gandhiji's ideas of 'basic-training' and he started providing training along its lines. To him, education meant the youngsters becoming cultured, neat, and healthy, and developing a capacity to stand economically on their own two feet. The youngsters who attended the school began to be drawn to Peter's ideas. Peter sincerely desired their progress and this touched their heart. Peter's method as well as teaching competence fired their enthusiasm.

One night, after finishing school, Peter started for the garden. Three hoodlums brandishing knives attacked him from behind. Peter could not recognize them in the dark, as they were masked. They warned Peter at the point of a knife that if he did not leave the slum in eight days he would be finished. Peter was momentarily stunned, but he was not paralyzed by fear. The hoodlums ran off. After Peter recovered his composure, he sat on a bench in the garden next to the factory. Shortly Shridhar came by. Peter laughed and said, "Chum! Just fifteen minutes back Mr. God sent His angels to fetch me; but they found me too heavy and so they just left me here!"

Shridhar stared blankly at Peter. But after he heard Peter's story Shridhar was adamant that Peter must leave his house in eight days. Those who had come to warn Peter were slum hoodlums. They trapped innocent children for use in their liquor and smuggling rackets. What would happen to their businesses if children became educated and well-behaved, and capable of taking up respectable vocations?

Peter contacted Mumbai's police commissioner. He recounted the entire episode. He also showed him his Canadian passport and asked him for his protection. The commissioner assured Peter that a plain-clothed policeman would constantly be with him.

This was the sixth day after the gangsters' warning. During those six days Peter contacted a large number of persons. Peter organized a public meeting in the nearby garden on the seventh day. At first, two representatives of the slum described the good work Peter was doing for the slum's uplift. Then Peter got up. "I have left the comforts of Canada to live amongst you because I have affection and concern for you. I am willing to share the education I got there with anyone amongst you who wants it. I have no desire except that you become respectable citizens and that your lives are enriched. For this work the hoodlums of the slum have threatened to kill me. My life is in your hands. I will not run away out of fear."

Peter was a favourite of the people of the slum. But after that day's public meeting he became virtually a leader. After the meeting was over, the earnest youngsters got together to discuss what was needed to be done in the slum, and how. The youngsters decided on a campaign of slum rejuvenation. The cleanup of the slum began the next day. Peter felt certain that these young torch-bearers would not stop until they achieved their goals.

Late at night Peter and Shridhar were sitting on the bench in the garden. Peter saw from Shridhar's drawn face that Shridhar was upset, and he tried hard to make him talk. Shridhar's lips were trembling with emotion, but he remained silent. "Perhaps I may die tomorrow . . ." Peter tried to joke about the threat to his life. But he could not complete the sentence because Shridhar's pent up feelings erupted and poured down from his eyes. Peter tenderly put his hand on his shoulder. Shridhar took Peter's hand in his and said, "Peter! If you do not go by tomorrow morning, I will personally drag you to the train and push you into it."

"Nobody is going to kill me. I am not afraid so why are you losing heart?"

"If you do not go by tomorrow morning, I shall go away for ever."

"I can only go if I leave early tomorrow morning without meeting anybody—but if I do this everybody will think that Peter ran away because of the threat."

"I shall tell the truth to everybody. You do not know these gangsters. They have knifed so many people!"

Shridhar was very firm and Peter had to leave before the day broke. The darkness helped to hide their pain from each other.

Peter used to write to me from India regularly and in detail, about what he was doing and how he was growing as a person. I also used to reply immediately and give him the news of Canada. For the last three months, there were no news from Peter. I was thinking of him when the doorbell rang. I looked through the 'magic eye.' It was Peter! There was no end to my amazement. He stormed in as soon as I opened the door. He sat in the chair, fingering his prickly beard. He announced, "Back to the pavilion."

"You are a modern Sindbad. Today you are here, and tomorrow you may be off on a voyage. What will you have, Peter?"

"Fresh air and tender love!" He threw open all the windows.

"Do you still remember that sage?"

"If I had wings I would fly there right now."

He said he was in a hurry and he would visit at leisure in a few days. Then he ran off as if he was trying to catch a moving bus.

A month later it was 'Janmashtami,' Krishna's birthday. I thought of going to the Hare Krishna temple. There would be service at midnight and then the breaking of the fast. And the food-mountain! It would be fun watching all these. It was midnight when I reached there. A Canadian devotee with a shaven head, a long shikha[9] sticking out from it, and wearing a silk dhoti was singing "Jaya Jagadeesha Hare, peela pitambar dhari."

He held a silver platter with a lamp on it. Canadian devotees, both male and female, were standing around him and clapping and singing. As soon as the service was over the person turned his face from the icon of Krishna to our side . . . and I screamed, "Peter!"

Peter raised his hand in benediction and signaled to me to keep quiet. After the ceremony of 'Nandotsav' he came and sat by my side and said gravely, "In two months I got fed up with my monotonous life. The clock would wake me up in the morning and I would get up—brush my teeth—take breakfast—get to work—return—watch TV with the family—then night. I became a machine."
"In India were you doing without brushing your teeth or bathing or getting ready or eating?"
"There I used to enjoy all these chores!"
"Then why did you return?"
"Perhaps service to Krishna had remained to be performed!"
"How did you get into the Hare Krishna fold?"
"Two or three of my friends joined here. I have faith in neither Krishna nor any other god; but I wanted a feel of rituals and to find out whether they do any good!"

Peter was fed up after three months of staunch brahminical rites. These rituals seemed worthless in comparison to the serenity and truth he had experienced in his stay with the sage.

A few days later I met Peter on Ste. Catherine Street. It was just as well that Peter pulled my braids from behind to stop me—because I could not have recognized the Peter I saw. He was in a classy suit and tie, with high heeled shoes and a stylish hair-cut!

"Peter! How many guises you take!"

---

9 tuft of hair on the head

"Currently I am an executive sales manager in IBM. Is the manager presentable in this outfit?"
"You look grand in any role you care to play!"

We both laughed. He glanced at his watch, saying "I must leave," and he quickly disappeared into the crowd.

Peter would get so engrossed in his work that failure would have to back down. In one year the company's sales of machines increased so much that the boss became a fan of Peter. He raised Peter's pay and promoted him. Peter's parents were relieved that finally their wayward son had settled down.

But in a short while Peter had understood the warp and woof of this business, and his mind was now seeking fresh pastures. He craved a new adventure.

The next day he went to his boss's cabin. Like detonating fire-crackers he told his boss: "Please get somebody else for my position."
The boss was stunned.
"Why? Is your salary inadequate? Or, do you have a better offer from somewhere else?"
"This job has become too routine for me. I have learnt whatever was worth learning. Now I will not continue in this job."
"Consider the scope you have for getting ahead here. In two years you could reach the top!"
"Here I won't get to the top I want to reach; but I will certainly continue until you find a replacement."

Peter shook hands, expressed regrets, and left the cabin.

Peter's parents sat at the dining table with long faces that night. Peter tried to talk to them a number of times; but by remaining mute both expressed bitter opposition to Peter's leaving his job. Finally, the mother broke the silence with sobs.

"We had hoped that you would look after us in our old age. But you roam around like a vagabond." The mother got up from the table and went to her room.

"When will you grow up?" The father spoke with a trembling, emotion-laden voice. Peter lovingly put his arms around his father's shoulders and said, "I am just 23; why should I tether myself to just one job?"

To Peter a static life was death. Peter would see a flower and wonder how it slept, fed, communicated. How would it suffer when it was plucked? He would want to become a flower and experience its life. He felt like becoming everything under the sun. Peter often used to dream about changing his body. If we were to list his dreams he would be found carousing in everything ranging from rocks to the living world's insects, fish, birds and animals. He would sometimes become a brahmin, sometimes a king, and sometimes a pall-bearer! How could this multi-tinted Peter take on just one shade? He did not want to pacify his parents with a lie that he was going to 'settle down' into a respectable rut and live like a machine. For hours Peter very gently explained to them what was in his mind. The parents felt a bit relieved.

For quite some time Peter had wanted to become a beggar and experience the hardships of a beggar's life. He felt an intense desire to test himself—could he live without any support at all? In the slum he could rely on Shridhar and his employer. After the school started Shridhar's employer had given Peter a small but comfortable room in the factory. In the pocket was a goodly fund of Canadian dollars. But suppose he had nothing except the clothes he was wearing and his two hands and feet, he was in an unfamiliar environment where he could count on nobody's help, and he had to fill his stomach by extending his arms for alms? In that stark world how long would he last? It was impossible to do this experiment in Montreal because there, if you do not have any means of support, the government provides maintenance. Who would beg in such a situation? And if one did beg, he would be thought insane and hauled off by the police! For this experiment our hero decided to return to India. It was not possible to give this reason to the parents and so he concocted one that they would find acceptable.

"I have not met my Indian friends for a long time. And Mr. Bannerji and Saloni will be happy because the last time I could not stay much with them. And then I badly need some change." The parents did find it difficult to swallow all this, but once Peter had made a decision what could they do? The parents went to the airport to see him off; but this time none of the three experienced the pangs of separation they had experienced the first time.

This time Saloni came to receive Peter at Delhi's Palam airport. The twenty years old Saloni was wearing white chudidar, white kurta, and a red bandhani dupatta. Her long, black, cascading hair reached down to her waist and spread like a fan over her entire back. She had a lustrous dark complexion and a graceful, curvaceous figure. When she walked she looked like a frond swaying in the breeze. Peter was sauntering absent-mindedly. Someone covered his eyes from behind. Peter caressed the fingers, and gauged the loveliness of the figure. He pretended not to recognize Saloni in order to get additional time for the feel of those silken fingers. "So you have already forgotten me!" Saloni said warmly and removed her fingers from Peter's eyes. Hand in hand the two got into the car and went home.

Peter stayed with Mr. Bannerji and Saloni for a fortnight. With them he visited Agra, Fatehpur-Sikri and a number of nearby places.

Peter kept fifty rupees with him and gave the rest to Saloni for safe-keeping. Mr. Bannerji had gone to the office and Saloni to her college. Peter left a note that he would return in about a week or two and that they should not worry about him. He departed for his experiment. At Delhi railway station he got a ticket for Mathura, and sat down in the train. Just before Mathura he went to the cloakroom, took out an ochre-coloured lungi[10] and a shirt, and put them on. He had not shaved in any case for quite a while. Peter got off at Mathura and walked to Vrindavan on foot. He put the rupees he had kept for his return to Delhi in the pocket of his shirt.

A red car came to a halt near a temple while he was watching the evening stoop over the banks of the Jamuna River. Three gentlemen and two ladies got out of the car and started freely distributing bananas and a fried snack. Some of the beggars changed their locations to get the goodies

10 A loose fitting garment worn on the lower part of the torso

twice. Only the last few bananas remained. Peter pushed himself towards the car. When the gentlemen and the ladies returned from the temple and were about to get into the car, Peter stood near the car's door as if guarding it, begging bowl in hand. His head was bowed in shame. One lady put the remaining bananas in Peter's begging bowl. Peter pressed his palms together in gratitude.

Whenever Peter extended his hand for alms he would feel acute shame. Also, he found it very difficult to live homeless on the road. Despite exhaustion from wandering for alms the whole day, at night he would turn and twist and struggle to fall asleep. As soon as he fell asleep he would wake up agitated, scratching the hives created by mosquito bites. In the naked heat of the afternoon, he would remember his cool, carpeted bedroom in Montreal.

Begging would sometimes yield money, sometimes food. The food was mostly dry and stale. While swallowing morsels he began to appreciate the importance of strong teeth and saliva. In Montreal he practically swallowed his greasy meals!

One day Peter could not get up due to several days of exhaustion and sleeplessness. Pilgrims were feasting on bhajias[11] and laddoos[12] under a nearby banyan tree. A little girl brought over to Peter a large packet of leftovers. Peter felt like a reposing lion that gets a meal of venison without any effort. He accepted the packet and quickly polished off the food.

What the tongue accepted the stomach rejected. From that afternoon to the night he suffered from agonizing spasms in his stomach. Late at night he began to vomit and pass stools. He spent the night moaning in pain. Peter had become unconscious by morning, smeared with his vomit and faeces. Flies swarmed on his face and body. He remained like this for many hours.

The driver of a municipal jeep stopped by, thinking Peter was dead. But finding him still alive, he drove off. After some hours a group of monks of the Ramakrishna Mission passed by. Out of a sense of duty they put

11 Vegetables fried in chick pea flour
12 Sweet balls made of ghee, sugar and flour

Peter in a tonga[13] and took him to a municipal hospital. Peter regained consciousness after two days of treatment. He was shocked to find himself in a hospital. Puss-filled boils from his scratching the mosquito bites covered his body. He felt a mighty desire to find out how he looked in the mirror; but he did not have the strength to walk up to the bathroom mirror. Realizing that he no longer could take the hardships of a beggar's life, he got a telegram sent to Mr. Bannerji to request him to come and get him.

Peter was asleep from sedation when Saloni reached the hospital in her car. Saloni was in agony when she saw Peter's condition. Mr. Bannerji had gone to Mumbai, and Saloni had read Peter's cable. She decided to go to Mathura by car. She sent off the driver for tea and she sat on Peter's bed. She began to caress his head. Peter's face lit up when he recognized the touch. Opening his eyes Peter saw Saloni's muffled sobbing. He held her hands in affection. What more could be done on a bed surrounded by so many patients? With the doctor's permission Peter left, assisted by the driver and Saloni.

Sitting side by side they began to talk.
"Why did you leave without telling me?"
"Would you have allowed me to go if I had told you?"
"Why were you so keen to leave me?"
"It was not that I wanted to leave you, Saloni! But I like to experience what others feel and I wanted to experience what a beggar feels."
"Were you really begging all these days?" Saloni shuddered as she asked the question.
"Shall I tell you the truth? The hardships of a beggar are utterly cruel; but in any intense experience there is a special charm. Although my body suffered gravely I could take the pain. I could feel peace as soon as I remembered the sage of Jamnotri."
"Are you used to hardships from childhood?"
"Not at all. I have been brought up in great comfort, and I also prefer comfort. But I learned to be patient after I met the sage. I learned to keep my cool in any adverse circumstances."

13 A horse-drawn buggy

Saloni felt a rush of admiration for this young man who was constantly probing the limits of his being and becoming.

Both had experienced warm feelings for one another when Peter had come to India for the first time; but now they felt that it was love. Peter decided to ask Mr. Bannerji for permission to marry Saloni. Peter made the proposal. Mr. Bannerji scratched his head and sighed. Mr. Bannerji was an outspoken person, so he told him bluntly: "You are a vagabond. You don't have any job. How will you look after my daughter? Go to Montreal and show me that you can do something. Then we can talk of marriage."

Peter's face fell. But he felt that if he were Saloni's father he would have said the same thing.

That year Saloni completed a B.A. in psychology. The psychology department at McGill University in Montreal is outstanding, and Peter expressed the wish that Saloni should do her masters degree there. Her father asked, "Where will she stay?"
"In the hostel. And if you permit it, in my house."
"How much would it cost for her study?" Mr. Bannerji asked, making mental calculations.
"I will earn and pay for her education," Peter said firmly.

The daughter was so insistent that the father had to give in.

Mr. Bannerji had sent details to his friends, Mr. and Mrs. Gupta. Peter's parents came to receive their son and their future daughter-in-law. They were delirious. Again and again they hugged Peter and Saloni.

Peter now studies business management in McGill University's evening programme. During the day he teaches in a primary school. Before taking this job, he had come to see me. I had returned home from college and I was leafing through a newspaper. War . . . war . . . war! Clashes erupting everywhere! Disoriented and in despair, I was seeking a ray of hope. Just then the doorbell rang. Who was visiting me at this grim time, I grumbled to myself. I opened the door. Peter entered, laughing loudly.

Someone covered in a white sheet from head to foot glided in behind him. Peter guided the person to the centre of the drawing room. I stared blankly.

"Let me show you a wonder from India!" Saying this he jerked off the sheet and Saloni and Peter salaamed low to me in Muslim style! We all laughed and laughed. There was instant merriment wherever there was Peter! He wanted to have two references for the school job; and he had come to ask my permission to give my name as a referee. He also wanted to know more about the school from me because I had taught there earlier. The principal was a friend of mine. I called him the next day and gave him Peter's background. Peter got the job.

Within a week Peter started teaching. Within three months the kids began to regard Peter as a super-teacher. Peter provided such fresh and unusual points of view that their enthusiasm zoomed. Peter taught there for two years. Saloni got her masters degree in psychology.

Now Peter and Saloni are husband and wife. Dr. Gupta and Danielle have the warmth of not one but two off-springs.

Peter and Saloni want to start an experimental school for creative children, without walled classes and a formal, published syllabus. The child would itself determine what it would like to study during the year. The teacher would discuss with the child the books that it may need, the place it would be able to get the books from, and the experts it may need to consult and how it may contact these experts. The child would be its own teacher. The teacher would provide only assistance. Peter believes that the minds of students fall victims to the dated, stale lectures given by teachers in conventional schools and colleges, and therefore remain in a state of eclipse. Peter and Saloni are shaping this experimental school.

Peter sought my help in this effort: "Hello! This is the principal of Rachana School. Is Mrs. Jai there?"
"This is Mrs. Jai. What can I do for you?"
"Kindly give up your ordinary college job and join my supreme school."

Peter said this in a fake voice. I could not recognize Peter—as it is, I have difficulty in recognizing people from their voices. I put down the receiver, thinking the caller was a prankster.

The doorbell rang in about fifteen minutes. It was Peter! "It is a crime not to talk properly on the phone and make some one needlessly come all the way", he said, without looking at me. He talked with his hands in his pockets, as if addressing an imaginary audience! We discussed the school's management for an hour.

Peter and Saloni's school is tops in Montreal. But can even God divine when Peter may set off for his next voyage?

RAMADI

"Ramadi! O Ramadi!" Wouldn't you think, from the way she was summoned, that Ramadi was a domestic servant? No! Actually Rama was Champama's elder daughter. Three or four minutes passed. The mother again bellowed. A thin, fifteen year old Rama, with lowered eyes, entered the kitchen. She started chopping vegetables even before being ordered. Her heart fluttered at the prospect of being pelted with the mother's choicest abuses. "Have you sprained your waist that it took you so long to come? Or were you rummaging through your tomes?" On receiving no answer, she steamed: "Wretched girl, don't you have a tongue?" She strongly felt like slapping Rama; but Rama was not near enough, and the mother's hands were busy making chapattis; so thrashing Rama was not feasible. But Champa found her day incomplete without giving at least one whack on Rama's back.

The family was large, and so Champa and her elder sister-in-law Manju daily prepared a mountain of chapattis. Champa had two daughters—Rama, and her younger sister Rita. Manju had seven sons. Like blocks of different heights, all were of different statures and ages. Champa's husband Virji was a clerk in an insurance company. Manju's husband Khimji ran a grocery store, and all his seven sons contributed their mites to the running of the store. Dhuliben, the mother-in-law of Champa and Manju, was still alive. However, her senses had got numbed years earlier. But that skeleton of stout bones still breathed. The two sons spent not even a minute with the mother. Champa and Manju served their mother-in-law, but openly showed their resentment. The sun of the two women always rose and set in the kitchen. At noon the two napped for an hour. Early evening was the hour of gossip with neighbours.

Rama was not attractive. She was thin, with no figure worth noticing, sparse hair, dull complexion, slightly stooping gait, and sunken but large, almond-shaped eyes. One hardly heard her voice. She kept mum unless she was made to speak.

The younger sister Rita—coquettish, with a cheeky tongue, shiny, abundant hair, a fine figure, and lustrous skin—was seductive. She knew well the tricks for charming others. After dinner, as soon as her father sat on the swing, she would run to bring him fragrant paans[14] and his snuff box. Her labours were modest, but the way she ran about and chattered, everybody would think she carried the house on her shoulders. She was everyone's pet. Rita was always at odds with her elder sister. She was an expert at getting Rama a scolding by complaining about her to her mother, aunt, and father. Rita was weak at studies. For the past two years she had been languishing in the seventh standard. It was hard for her to memorize references to contexts, and who said what to whom in her language and history texts. But she never faltered in remembering film dialogues, and in recalling which actor said what to which actress in which Bollywood movie!

Manju's sons ranged, in age, from twelve to eighteen. All seven and Rita recounted film dialogues to one another with great relish. In this house Rama was a lost soul. Rama did not stand first in the class; but she had a thirst for knowledge, and patience to probe into the depths of things. In the class Rama hesitated in answering questions put to her, and at times she trembled and stuttered. Most teachers had not noticed this, since she was not their favourite. In her class, a couple of boys who fluently answered teachers' questions were favourites. Rama did well in written exams; but, due to fright, she fared disastrously in the orals. Rama's face was a plaster-cast of seriousness. Due to her stolid, unvarying expression, her face looked like a grim portrait hung on a wall. She never shared her concerns and anxieties with anyone at home. She had no friends because she was not sociable. Sometimes Rama felt so suffocated—as if somebody had pushed her into a vessel full of steam and tightly closed its lid! When the suffocation became unbearable she would get into the bathroom, lock the door, and weep silently.

14 green, chewable, leaves that are usually spiced

A new teacher had arrived at the school that year. Her name was Daminiben. With her entry the school's dull mien acquired sheen. She was comely, with a pointed nose, long, dark, prancing eyes, sensuous lips, and skin that was radiant like the shine on freshly polished vessels. Her figure was well-proportioned but a bit rounded, and she adorned it very elegantly indeed. The students and the teachers daily speculated on how Daminiben would be dressed and how she would look when she arrived at the school. Temperamentally, she was both serious and playful. Normally she bounced around like a ball, though at times her face was tense, as if stretched out on hooks. Daminiben had a sharp mind and she had read widely; but she did listen patiently to others views. However, if a mediocre person fancied himself to be extraordinary and locked horns with her over an issue, she could tear him apart with the ferocity of her feline claws-like logic. Many feared her for this intimidating side of hers. Even to her superiors she proffered opinions with complete frankness. She loved to teach. Her job was but an excuse to indulge in this passion of hers. With the skills of an expert potter she dexterously shaped the personalities of her students.

Rama was in the tenth standard, and Daminiben was her class teacher. It did not take Daminiben long to discern Rama's true nature. She started paying more attention to Rama once she realized that the dumb-looking Rama wore many masks. Daminiben would persistently question Rama. Whenever Rama fumbled she would help her to proceed further. Raising a shepherd's staff, as it were, Daminiben would turn ferociously on any one daring to poke fun at Rama's stammering. The classmates kept mum out of fear of Daminiben's wrath; but once she left, they dismembered Rama with epithets like 'stuttering runt', 'pole', and 'matchstick'. Then Rama's eyes would drown in tears.

Rama found shelter under Daminiben's canopy. She felt much less scared in Daminiben's class. On the way to the school, she would often pluck a flower from a garden, and secretly pass it to Daminiben. Daminiben would sniff it, toss her head merrily, and praise the flower and Rama's loving gesture. Rama's heart would spill over its banks.

From childhood, Rama was addicted to reading. By now she had devoured heaps of storybooks. She suffered with the aches of their characters. In her dreams a collage would form of the images of the reality of her life and the lives of these characters. Sometimes she would wake up with a scream. But no hand ever caressed her head to calm her howling terrors.

These days the contours of Rama's dreams have undergone a sea change. She keeps shifting from one colourful dream to another, like an unfolding roll of printed cloth. These days she eagerly waits for the night so that she can strut about in the fairyland fair of her rainbow dreams. Rama craves to paint this dream world of hers. If permitted, she would surely cover every inch of her home's walls with these wondrous paintings. But were she to paint at home, her parents and sister would pick her apart. Where can she paint? From where can she get the money for paper, colours, and brush?

One day Rama chanced upon a twenty-rupee note on the way to her school. She looked around stealthily. She picked it up, but with trepidation. Nobody had noticed. She did feel a pang of remorse. But the way for her to paint seemed to open up. On reaching the school she bought drawing paper and a box of colours from the bookstore. During the recess, not having any friends in her class, Rama used to have her snacks alone under a large mango tree in the school's grounds. But today she forgot lunch, and instead she went to the drawing classroom with her paper and colours. She sat in a corner to escape being observed by loitering students. She started painting the prior night's still fresh dream with total concentration.

When the bell rang for the end of the recess, Rama climbed upon a chair and hid the incomplete painting on a high cupboard. For three weeks Rama kept to this routine. Now the painting was nearly finished. One day she was late for class in her desire to complete it. Daminiben said nothing to Rama. Daminiben called Rama after the class was over. She asked her why she was late for class. Rama broke down and told her the truth. After the school was over Daminiben took Rama to the drawing classroom.

On seeing the painting Daminiben was struck dumb. A large lake was set amidst green trees. The sunlight filtered down from the foliage and shimmered on the water. Five fish were standing in the water, with human faces and piscine torsos. Each had two arms near the head. A majestic fish in the centre sat on a splendid throne adorned with tiny multi-hued fish. She looked like a queen. A fish on her left was putting a crown on her head and the one on the right was fanning her with a fan made of peacock feathers. Such was the force of the colours that even an art expert would have gaped in admiration.

Daminiben warmly embraced Rama. "Rama, do you paint at home?" Rama looked down and started to scratch the ground with her toe-nail. She tried once or twice to say something but tears choked her. Daminiben began to caress Rama's head affectionately. This was the first time Rama had experienced such a gentle, soft touch. She felt like seizing Daminiben's hand and gluing it permanently to her head.

"You are not able to paint at home? They scold you?" In a breaking voice Rama painted the grim reality of her family life. Shadows gathered on Daminiben's face.
"Has your mother never showered affection on you?"
"If slaps can be called affection she showers it on me everyday", Rama said bitterly.
"Does your mother shower affection on your younger sister?"
"No, she does not shower affection; but she often says that she is her favourite daughter."

It was a wonder to Rama that Daminiben had heard her story with so much patience.

"I will tell your mother to send you to my house. Will you come?" Countless 'yesses' tumbled out from Rama's eyes.

"Rama! Will you give this painting to me?"

In her emotional excitement, Rama got so paralyzed that she could not even say "Yes". Stumbling around in the dark for years, Rama suddenly experienced a radiant guidance. She felt like tightly hugging Daminiben.

But before she could express her feelings, she suppressed them from habit.

After coming home, Daminiben stuck Rama's painting on the wall opposite her bed. For days, Daminiben kept deciphering the Rama in the painting.

One day Daminiben met Rama's art teacher in the recess. "Madhubhai! I would like to see Rama's paintings that she has made this year. Could you please show them to me?"
"Which Rama?"
"The one who is in my class. The one in standard 10A."
"Oh that skinny one? What is there to see in her paintings?"
"Please forgive me, Madhubhai! You may be an art teacher; but I am afraid you have no feel for art." Daminiben threw the sentence like a spear.

Madhubhai rummaged through a cupboard and threw down Rama's paintings on the table.

"Sorry for the trouble. I will return them tomorrow." Daminiben left without even a glance at Madhubhai.

At home that evening, Daminben examined Rama's paintings with care. In her paintings there was a heavy use of black, grey, coffee brown, white, and red. There were no irises in the eyes of the people she had painted. These characters with hollow eyes were eloquently mute. No colours chirped in the birds, flowers, or butterflies Rama had painted. Despair brooded over all the paintings—except in her last painting. What a colour-fest it was!

On Sunday morning at ten Daminiben arrived at Rama's residence. Rama was taken aback on opening the door. Anxiety flooded the natural creases on her forehead. Would her parents welcome properly a person who was her beloved? Rama tenderly made Daminiben sit on a chair in the living room.

There was a balcony adjoining the living room. Rama's father was slowly swaying back and forth on a swing. He was frequently pushing into a nostril a twisted corner of his dhoti to induce sneezing. Rama said, with lowered head and tremulous voice, "My class teacher has come to meet you."
"You must have made a fool of yourself! What was the fault this time?"

Before Rama could say anything he rose from the swing and came into the drawing room. Mother came from the kitchen. Greetings were exchanged, and Daminiben was requested to take a seat.

Daminiben started speaking: "I must congratulate the parents of such a nice, cultured girl." The parents expected a long list of complaints. Ears unused to hearing Rama's praise were shocked. Rita came over, swatting her wet hair for drying them.

"Namaste teacher," she said, a bit affectedly, and sat some distance away. Her face twisted with envy when she heard the litany of praise for Rama, and that too from her class teacher! A bit overwhelmed by the lavish praise, the mother asked Rita to prepare tea, instead of giving the customary order to Rama to prepare it. Rita got up to make tea, but not without a grimace. After tea and some chitchat Daminiben got up to go. "Oh! I forgot to mention something! Could you please send Rama to my place next Sunday?" The parents agreed. "I live next to the school—the name of the bungalow is Smriti." Daminiben bade goodbye and left.

After Daminiben left, as if in shock, everyone was silent for a while. Rita broke the silence: "This teacher is so silly." In this house in fifteen years Rama had never answered anyone back. But that day, trying to quell her crimson fury, she said, "Daminiben is our school's best teacher—and don't you call her names in my presence."

"Oho! You have to take the side of your admirer!"

The father took a pinch of snuff and mildly reproved Rita. Annoyed, Rita stormed down the stairs to visit her neighbourhood friend.

Daminiben's visit had a definite effect. Insults to Rama declined.

The whole week Rama thought of nothing but what she would do the coming Sunday. She would wake at dawn, bathe, put on the newly stitched, red printed chudidar-kurta, and go to Daminiben's house. She would discuss so many things with her!

Sunday arrived. At nine, after informing her parents, Rama winged to Daminben's residence. Daminiben opened the door even before Rama rang the bell. After a chat, Daminiben put a cardboard box in Rama's hands: "Open and see what's inside!" Rama quickly opened it. Out came bottles of colour and brushes of all sizes. "These are all for you," Daminiben said, softly like a petal. Choked with emotion, Rama could say nothing for some moments.

"Why are you doing so much for me?"
"Because I like you so much."

Rama felt like storing for ever in her heart the bouquet of these moments. Daminiben rose to give her some drawing paper.

"Now sit down and paint."

Daminiben went to her room and started writing a letter to her parents. Her father was a tycoon in Uganda. The mother had a B.A. in economics from Elphinstone College in Mumbai, and half of her husband's success was certainly due to her. Both had raised little Damini like a son. She was not denied anything. At 17, after passing the Senior Cambridge examination, she was sent off to Mumbai for studies. Indians in Africa generally have some relatives in Mumbai or Vadodara. Damini was sent to Mumbai so that relatives could keep an eye on her and help her out in a tight corner.

Damini fell in love with a young man studying with her. They agreed to marry. But one day he just disappeared, never to return. There was not even a note from him. She languished for a while; but not for long. Damini's buoyant, green temperament again began to assert itself.

Damini had wanted to be a teacher even as a child. Her favourite game with her girl friends was to play the game of 'teacher'. No one but Damini would, of course, become the teacher. The others would act as pupils. After getting her M.A. Damini became Daminiben for students. Daminiben was offered a lecturer's post in her college but she wanted to teach in a school. "I would enjoy teaching those on the threshold of youth more than the fully grown steers of a college", she told the school principal during her interview.

By now Daminiben was around 35 and the parents were worried and unhappy that she was still a spinster. But she refused to see any 'boys'. And the parents knew that when Damini said no, she meant it.

Daminiben wrote regularly to her parents to keep them abreast of her news. The parents felt intimacy with their daughter through her words of affection.

"The lunch is ready", the servant announced. Daminiben rose from her chair and went and stood behind Rama. Rama was engrossed in her painting.

"Rama! Your paintings these days are entirely different from your earlier ones, as if they have been painted by two entirely different persons!" Rama said nothing.

At the dining table Rama asked hesitantly, "Why do I falter while speaking? No other student in my class falters so much!"
"You are so afraid of others."
"Don't other kids have as much fear as I have?"
"Who else has been trampled upon so much by parents?"

"I don't understand anything; but I want to get rid off my stuttering. Everybody starts laughing the moment I get up to speak."

The hour of the evening advanced to the threshold. It was eight when Daminiben dropped Rama home. So envious was Rita that for half-an-hour Rita revolved around Rama, trying to ferret out what Rama did all day. Disappointed at Rama's brief, non-committal answers, Rita fell asleep while turning over the photos of actors and actresses in Filmfare. Rama remained awake, re-living the dialogues of the day.

People at home often used to make critical comments about Rama's appearance. She was used to epithets like 'twiggy', 'witchy', 'raggy'. But inside her she used to shrivel whenever these were hurled at her. The next Sunday, as soon as she went to Daminiben's house she asked, "Am I very ugly?"
"Who told you that?"
"Everybody at home says so. At school also everybody thinks I am ugly."
"Even by mistake you cannot be called ugly."
"But why should I appear ugly to others if I am not ugly?"
"You don't have self-confidence."
"Rita—my sister—does she look pretty because she has self-confidence?"
"She is certainly pretty. But if she did not have self-confidence, she wouldn't look as attractive as she does."
"Then I . . ."
"Only through self-confidence a person attracts others. If you do not respect yourself, how would others respect you?"
"What have I got that I should respect myself?"
"Just you look within! You have patience! Amazing endurance! Seldom does one your age have such a thinking capacity as you have! You are an extraordinary painter! How pure you are! There is no deceit in you! Tell me, do all these virtues count for nothing? If you do not seem attractive, despite all these qualities, the reason is your lack of self-confidence."

The caravan of conversations continued rolling until evening. Rama went home. She washed her face in the bathroom. While wiping her face she looked at it intently. The curtain of pale-dull-dark persona moved aside, and Rama saw her self splashed with colours. She saw two new eyes sprout within her old eyes. She recognized them. They were saying, "Rama, you are attractive." Rama gazed at her new eyes and said, "From now on I will believe only you."

Rama looked into the mirror and carried on imaginary conversations with real life persons. The Rama of the mirror sometimes played the role of Mother, sometimes of Father, sometimes of her aunt, and sometimes of Rita. Using their gestures and mannerisms she scolded herself. Seizing the fringes of her self-confidence, she answered them back. As soon as she got stuck like a gramophone's needle in a defective groove, she began all over again her intended response. Thus did the pages of days turn one by one.

Just a few days earlier, when Rama wore a kurta stitched from a yellow Marwari bandhani[15], Mother said, "This colour suits Rita." Straightening her stooping shoulders, Rama said, "I like myself in this colour." Mother stared wide-eyed at her.

The results of the All India Youth Painting Competition held six months earlier were announced. Rama bagged the first prize. The principal of the school came to her class specially to make the announcement. The Rama of old would have suppressed her happiness. But this time happiness suffused her face. Nobody cared a damn about her triumph. Two students sitting behind her said, loudly enough for Rama to hear, "This Damudi hung the prize on Ramadi's neck; otherwise this skinny-ninny can barely draw a straight line." Rama's bliss was shattered. Her limbs went limp as if her blood was sucked out by leeches. She felt faint and her head sagged. The principal asked the students to give Rama a hand. The applause was faint. Rama felt devastated.

Rama's eyes were red from crying. After much thought Rama resolved that she would not go to college in this town. Her family members, fellow students, and relatives had all pigeonholed Rama. However Rama might change, their image of Rama would remain unchanged. She could create a positive image of herself only in a new environment where nobody from her past knew her.

It was Sunday. At eight in the morning Rama arrived at Daminiben's residence. Daminiben agreed with Rama's resolve that she should leave the town; but she was unhappy at the thought of separation from Rama.

Like an ant that diligently gathers specks of food, Rama gathered courage for days. Her heart fluttered like a sari in a strong breeze when she approached her parents. With trepidation she expressed her wish to go to Vadodara to study in the fine arts college there.

15 a tie-and-die cloth

"What is the point of becoming a painter? You still don't know the ABC of cooking. We will be through once we fix you up with the son of Shamaldas Tanna. They are coming to see you in two-three days."
"I won't see the boy, Mother."
"Not see him? I will skin you alive!"

Rama slipped away just before the prospective bridegroom's arrival. Rita and the seven sons of Manju scoured all of Rama's haunts in vain.

At eight at night, a terrified and shriveled Rama returned home. She was hammered like a nail, drubbed like a soiled cloth, crushed like sugarcane. But throughout her ordeal Rama remained stoic like the Buddha. The parents never forgave Rama.

Rama's luck was in. She won Rs.10000 award in a youth painting competition organized by the Soviets. Taking advantage of this opportunity, Daminiben went to meet Rama's parents. After pleasantries Daminiben suggested that Rama should be allowed to go to the fine arts college in Vadodara.

"We don't want her to study any more. If we allow her she won't get a boy in our caste. And people in our caste would speak badly of us if we send her to another town", Rama's mother replied harshly.

"Don't you wish that your daughter becomes famous throughout India as a painter? And—it is Rama's life. Shouldn't you ask her what she wants to do?"

The father answered Daminiben's question with a war cry: "The girl is ours; we will act according to our wishes. What is there to ask the girl? The girl must accept whatever the parents decide. If we educate her so much that she becomes over-ripe, then who will select such unpalatable fruit? If no one marries her then we would have to endure her for life!"
"If she is such a burden to you I am willing to keep her", Daminiben said, slightly raising her voice.

From the time Rama had mentioned about wanting to go to college the atmosphere at home had turned explosive. That day Daminiben lit a matchstick. The mother gave a shove to Rama and said: "Get out if you want to go to college. This 'relative' of yours will keep you." The father seized Rama's hand and forcibly pushed her out of the door. Daminiben too got out in the nick of time. The door banged shut behind them. Her father roared, "Don't step into this house. We are writing you off."

With pounding hearts, the two sat on the stairs. They hoped that the door would open once tempers cooled. The babble of the whole home froze, eager to hear the descent of footsteps. For a while there was a wafer thin calm. Then the mother bellowed: "Coward! Why don't you go? Why are you sitting on the stairs?"

Four feet hurried down the stairs.

Daminiben initiated an effort to start a school in Vadodara with the help of Prince Ranjitsinh. Rama entered Vadodara's fine arts college. Once the two had settled down, Daminiben wrote to her parents:

> *Revered Mother and Father:*
>
> *Don't think that I have forgotten you because I am writing after a long time. I remain so happy because in my mind you are all the time with me.*
>
> *The special news is that I have become a mother without marrying. I have given birth to a child without becoming pregnant! My daughter weighs 40 kilos. Please come to see your grand-daughter as soon as you can. And plan to stay for a long period. Your grand daughter is pining for you. Let us meet soon.*
>
> *My respectful salutations,*
> *Damini*

These days Rama's cheeks are no longer hollow, and there is an effulgence on her face. Now she walks erect, her eyes aglow with the world's wonders. These days she, too, has forgotten the Rama of yore.

KARNA

A haveli[16] is sprawled in the center of a small town of Gujarat. No fancy filigree work or other ornamentation, but within it, like the leaves of a cabbage, are chambers within halls and within them still smaller enclosures.

The owner is Narmadashankar, the chief priest of the town, whose word is law when it comes to birth, death, and marriage functions. People bow to him for his piety, his fine temperament, and the sanctity of his word. Narmadashankar has a coppery complexion. No disease has yet laid him low. Slightly squat, and under forty, his round face is livened by piercing eyes and a pointed nose. His wife Laxmi is slim, and she looks soft and satiny. A chandla[17] graces her forehead like the rising sun. It is a mystery how and when her day rises and sets amidst all the chores of cleaning, cooking, tending to guests, raising kids, and maintaining relationships.

There is, however, ceaseless din in the haveli, as the neighbourhood children run amuck, turning it into a virtual carnival. The leader of the pack is Karna, the ten-year old son of the priest. He looks more like eleven or twelve, though. He has a resolute gait. The voice is still reedy; but it rings with determination. He is moon-faced like his father, and has the silken complexion of the mother. He has small but lustrous eyes. His eyebrows are frequently puckered in thought, and in relation to the face, he has a slightly extra long and wide nose. Karna certainly cannot be called handsome; but he has the bearing of a leader and a doer. The local kids have made him their captain, since he is not only adventurous and

16 An old-style Indian mansion

17 A round, red mark generally worn by married Hindu women

prankish, but also receptive and sensitive. He often concocts new games and gets them to play these after explaining their rules.

One day, for instance, Karna thought of making a raft for an excursion on the river. He got his whole gang to work. They peeled logs, cut them with a saw into boards, and nailed them together. On a full moon night the team carried snacks, got onto the raft, and floated down the river. They made merry with songs, jokes, and tomfoolery. The locality became listless on the day Karna was indisposed.

Karna regularly attended school; but the teacher would be talking about a Mughal emperor, and Karna would be contemplating some new mischief. The teacher would insist on rote learning and Karna would keep yawning. Once, the lesson was about the forest wealth of Gujarat. Karna listened attentively. Then the teacher made the children repeat after him the things that could be made out of trees and plants. Karna kept yawning and glancing out of the window. The teacher ordered him to stand up and reprimanded him: "You fellow there, have your lips been stitched? You think you know everything?"

"I am not proficient yet, but I am not silly like the rest. I can't keep on repeating the same thing." Teachers did feel annoyed with such stinging retorts, but who could punish the chief priest's son?

Karna would be all ears in the science class whenever the teacher described the body's anatomy. But he would shoot questions at the teacher like sten-gun fire: "Sir, why do we get an itch?" "Why do we belch?" "Why don't animals get tickled?"

"You must have tried to tickle many animals to know this! Which ones have you tickled?"
"Sir, I have experimented with dogs, cats, buffaloes, cows, squirrels, pigeons, crows, parrots—all sorts of creatures."

If the teachers had their way they would have driven Karna out of the school. At home, too, Karna often got into an altercation with his father.
"Father, why do we wear the sacred thread?"
"A brahmin must wear it."
"But what would happen if you don't wear it?"

"That would be a grave sin."
"What happens if you sin gravely?"

Narmadashankar would get exasperated with such a volley of questions. He would feel uncomfortable in giving answers and he would avoid being alone with Karna.

Years bounded away and Karna was now a youth. One day, while returning from the school, Karna saw a dead dog on the road. A multitude of flies was buzzing on the carcass and the stink was unbearable. Despite his revulsion, Karna itched to go near it. For a while, he struggled within to touch it or not to touch it. He would extend a finger and withdraw it. Finally, mobilizing his courage and taking a deep breath, he touched the dead dog. He wondered about the dog's heart. Would its skin be thicker than man's? To find answers he made a small cut into the carcass with his penknife. Then he tried deeper and larger cuts. Karna was fascinated. Karna surmised that the dog was run over, since its head was crushed, and the skin of the head was peeled off, revealing lumpy flesh. On seeing the dog's skull, he tried to understand its structure. Belatedly remembering home, he wiped his hands on the grass and ran towards home.

Red like hot iron, Narmadashankar was steaming towards him with long strides. "Where were you buried all this time?" Narmadashankar shouted, and gave him two-three sound slaps. Trembling, Karna told him what had transpired. Narmadashankar collapsed in shock onto the ground. The son of the community's priest soiling his hands inside a roadside carcass! The thought raised in his mind such turmoil of despair, fury, revulsion, and pain that he was immobilized for some moments. After regaining composure, he rapidly strode homeward with Karna.

For the first time in his life Narmadashankar entered his house trying to hide from his neighbours. He took a deep breath of relief that he had saved himself from the prying eyes of the town. There was a brief conversation between the husband and the wife, and Laxmi led Karna away for bathing and purification. Reciting the names of the holy rivers—Kaveri, Narmada, Ganga, and Yamuna—she thoroughly scrubbed him with soap. Finally, Narmadashankar recited mantras and sprinkled holy Ganga water on Karna's head. Karna could not understand the reason for his parents' agony. Karna wondered: "It would have been an evil deed had I killed a dog; but this dog was dead! If it is no sin to touch one's own body then why is it a sin to touch a dog's body?" After supper the parents lovingly cajoled the son to promise never to do this again. The promise was given in deference to the parents' sentiments, but hesitantly.

But three days later Karna found a dead rat in a corner of the house, and took him to a room on the terrace for dissection. He tried to understand the rat's anatomy. Afraid that he might get preoccupied too long, he wrapped the dismembered rat in a piece of paper and hid it in an alcove in the room. He went downstairs after cleaning his hands, but Laxmi saw some drops of blood on his shirt and screamed. That day the parents thrashed Karna. Then they both started weeping. "If you pile up corpses in a brahmin's house, who will accept my priesthood?" The father entreated. A torrent of tears poured out from Karna's eyes, too.

Karna got so fascinated by anatomy that as soon as he saw a dead insect, bird, or animal he would want to dissect it and peer inside. Karna was still the leader of the troop of tailless monkeys; but play had greatly abated. Two or three times he talked about anatomy to his gang to stoke their interest; but the members expressed utter revulsion. The children told their parents. The gossip spread, and eventually reached the ears of the priest and his wife.

Karna was their only child, their cynosure. Still, they began to take a dislike to him. Karna challenged their core values, and this was the source of their revulsion. To Narmadashankar, his priesthood was his whole existence. He believed that he was semi-divine since he was born in the highest caste, and that, too, in a priestly family. Karna often wondered whether anything would remain of his father's existence if his status as a brahmin priest was whisked away from him. Karna was now an adolescent; but he was mature for his age. He had the capacity to get to the roots of things. Suppose, he wondered, he was not Narmadashankar's son and nor a brahmin, he still would be the person known as Karna. His mind and his ideas were developing in such a way that others seemed by comparison to be ill-developed midgets.

The whole town now knew of Karna's passion. By now he had got used to his parents' thrashings. Kids were no longer to be seen in a mansion that once resounded with their squeals. Gradually he lost all his friends. He descended to the nadir in his parents' hearts, like a well's water in drought. The members of the community no longer gave to the priest the deference they used to give earlier. At times the son seemed a curse to the parents. Friendless, Karna would get lonesome like an unused well. Karna had love and sympathy for his parents. He understood their pain. But he was not prepared to accept that his brahminhood, his parents, or the people of the town should decide for him what he could or could not do.

The day came that was dreaded by both Karna and his father. An argument got out of hand and the father ordered the son to leave the house. Karna decided that he would not spend the next morning in that town. He left when it got dark. He walked on, like a wind that blows where nature wills it. He reached the railway station of a nearby town. He bought a ticket for Mumbai. The train arrived huffing and puffing, and he climbed into a compartment. He felt like an uprooted tree. Where would he go? Where would he stay? How would he live? He began to perspire. He took out his wallet. He had saved in it the money he had got as gifts from people on holy days. He counted it carefully. He had Rs.155.

The hustle and bustle of Mumbai's Bombay Central station woke Karna. He saw porters in red shirts and yellowed dhotis run about. The station overflowed with people. He got down and sat on a bench to observe the goings on. Hunger growled in his stomach, so he got to a food stall and had refreshments. He remembered the creamy milk tea made by his mother. He remembered his mother. He remembered his home. The stings of memories left numerous red hives on his mind.

An engine shrieked. A train approached, roaring, stunning the ears. It jerked to a halt. Passengers quickly poured out. The porters began to jostle for cartage. Soon the platform was empty. But two passengers were still standing on the platform, a bit distraught at not getting a porter. Karna thought, "Why not I carry their luggage?"

"May I carry the luggage?" Karna asked the passengers.

"Your porter number?"
"I am not a porter, but I will be able to carry the luggage." On putting the heavy bag on his head, he felt that his head would split. While carrying it to a taxi, many times he felt like flinging down the load and running off.

Over the next few days he got used to being a porter. He was repelled by the dirt, noise and congestion of the station. But where could he go in this maze of a city? On the station he could get a bath, wash clothes, get food, and earn. But to be able to stay there he had to earn the favour of the local bully, the porters, and the station's officials. For this he had to cringe before them, and pay their dues. He was unhappy at having to do things he disliked. But he was convinced that this situation was temporary, and this kept him going.

He could not get chummy with the other porters. In their moments of respite, the porters would gather in groups on the platform, extend their legs, smoke bidis[18], talk smut and laugh at inane jokes. In his free time Karna would instead borrow books from a bookstall. Girish, the owner of the bookstall had taken a fancy to him. In exchange, Karna did numerous chores for him. Girish came from a poor family and had to struggle hard before he got established in his trade. His life story of successful struggle invigorated Karna.

For quite some time Girish had been persuading Karna to leave being a porter and work for him in the bookstall. Karna finally agreed to this. Karna had a way of attracting customers. He observed the customer's dress and language, and judged his mental status and preferences. He then would tell the customer what book or magazine might meet the customer's need, and thus effect a sale. The sales went up. Karna got five rupees a day and the comfort and warmth of a friendship.

One evening, Karna was sitting on a bench in a garden outside the railway station, reading a science magazine. A dead crow fell in front of him, electrocuted by the wire of an electricity pole. Karna went over to investigate. Earlier, in the village, Karna had dissected a crow, but the

18 Cheap cigarette

crow here had a band of grey, and its beak was smaller and narrower—it seemed to be city bred! He got a strong itch to dissect the crow and examine its anatomy. He opened the shop and got out his bag of instruments. To escape prying eyes he went over to the parking lot, spread a newspaper between two cars, and sat down. In the neon light Karna carefully dissected the crow, took out its organs, and put them on the paper. He took out a notebook from his bag and painstakingly drew in it the outlines of the organs.

Just then a man dressed in suit and tie came to the car. Karna was totally absorbed in his work. He was on the point of asking Karna to move when his eyes fell on the very carefully drawn outlines of the organs. Karna closed his book and quickly began to pack up. The stranger, a doctor, was intrigued. He asked Karna to show him the notebook. Karna gave it, but with great diffidence. After carefully examining the book he looked sharply at Karna's face and demanded: "From whom did you learn to draw these?"
"I learnt myself," Karna said softly.
"And . . . this surgery—where did you learn?"

Surprised by Karna's answer, the doctor probed Karna about where he was staying and what he was doing. Doctor Bhagwati got into his car. Before driving off he gave his card to Karna and asked him to come to his office in the next two or three days. The car gone, Karna leaped about like a fount of joy. This was the first person to take interest in his work. Karna could not sleep. He kept being high on fantasies about the opening of a wonderful new portal.

Dr. Bhagwati was indeed impressed by Karna's determination and precision, his perseverance, and also his hunger for knowledge. Karna's eager face popped many times into his mind. Everyday Karna felt like meeting the doctor; but how would it look to go to somebody's place just after a brief meeting? A few days passed in this dilemma. But on the fourth day he decided that come what may, he would go to meet the doctor the next day. He began to muse about what the doctor would ask him and how he would answer.

He got up early the next day and scrubbed himself hard in the station's bathroom. He had got his hair cut the previous day. He had also washed his clothes and got them ironed by a roadside laundry man. He went to the waiting room and observed his face several times in the mirror.

It was four in the afternoon. He sought Girish's suggestions, and left after taking his permission. Asking directions and changing buses, he finally climbed the steps to Dr. Bhagwati's clinic at Opera House.

Patients were waiting. Not knowing what to do, for a while he just stood sheepishly. Then he sat hesitantly on the edge of a sofa. He was pretty exhausted getting to this place. Mumbai seemed like a vast labyrinth of tar strings, and like waves hurrying about in the sea, cars and buses raced everywhere. He would get so frightened while crossing a road that he would shut his eyes and run to the other side. During the next few minutes he would wipe away perspiration and try and slow down his pounding heartbeats. He was cast into a city of monstrous speeds. He felt like a satellite that has been shot into space without any control over its flight path.

After a while the doctor emerged from his cabin. Karna got up and pressed his palms together in greeting. "Sit down, I will call you later," the doctor said, and again went inside. One by one the patients were called in. Karna kept watching restlessly. Eventually, all the patients departed. At the thought that now he would be called in, his pulse accelerated like Mumbai's 'double-fast' suburban trains.

The doctor beckoned Karna inside his cabin. He asked him to take a chair. He questioned Karna about his parents, town, and education. The doctor felt no qualms about Karna. On hearing Karna's story the doctor's heart beat wildly. What talent!

"Do you want to work in my clinic?" Karna could not believe what he was hearing. The doctor asked again. Karna nodded his head vigorously. He perked up a little courage and asked what work he would be doing. "What sort of work do you want to do?" The doctor asked in turn. "Any work that can help me develop myself—and I would like to study half the time."

Karna was in the 11th standard of his school when he had left his town. "You can stay in my clinic. You have to receive calls, keep the clinic clean,

get the patients seated, send them in—these are your duties. The rest of the time you can study."
"How can I study without getting into a school?"
"All that will be arranged in due course."

The doctor gave the clinic's key to Karna, and explained to him how to lock and unlock it, how to dial numbers, how to receive calls, how to talk on the phone.

Karna began to live all alone in the clinic. Accustomed to being incessantly surrounded by people, Karna was frightened at this seclusion in a strange place. In his childhood he had heard many ghost stories and he began to remember these. Karna would shiver. He felt like taking refuge in the shelter of his mother's sari. As soon as he raised his hand to grasp the sari, it kept floating away from him. All night the light—and his eyes—were on. This went on for a few days. But then later, with increasing familiarity, he fell asleep as soon as he got into his bedding.

Karna now began to relish his daily routine. He got up at four in the morning and studied an English reader. Then he read stories in English. The doctor had given these books to him and had commanded: "You should know English well in six months." He looked up the meanings of unfamiliar words in the dictionary. At eight he did the exercises he had learnt in his school. Then, bath and breakfast—there was a fridge in the clinic in which the doctor used to keep milk, butter, bread, bananas, etc.

Karna read the newspaper every day and looked carefully for the photos of missing children. Deep down, he was hoping that his parents would publish his photo in the papers, with the message, 'You will not be scolded—come back from wherever you are—your mother has given up food', and so on. Not finding any reference to him in the paper, he would get dejected. After that, he would study according to the syllabus of the 11th standard. He would lunch at one in a restaurant downstairs.

He still had no friends. It was not feasible to visit Girish frequently. The neighbours thought of Karna as a servant and so boys from 'good' families did not befriend him. And how could Karna, of a respectable family, high ideals, and bright mind, get along with the servants of the locality? Lonely and frustrated, he would stare out of a window at the passing traffic.

For Karna, time ran golden from four in the afternoon to eight at night. He eagerly awaited this period from the morning. All sorts of patients came. He wrote their names on chits, and talked to them. At times Dr. Bhagwati would ask Karna to come into the cabin, show an X-ray against light, and explain anything odd in it. Karna was intensely interested in the names, symptoms, and diagnoses of diseases.

After some time, with difficulty Dr. Bhagwati got Karna enrolled in a nearby school. Karna would get back to the clinic at five. He enjoyed being with fellow pupils so much that exhilaration shone on his face. At the closing bell, when others were hurrying home, Karna would stroll, and be the last to emerge from the gates. His friends would chide him: "Normally you are off like a rocket, but how come you turn into a snail when leaving the school?" Karna felt bad. How to tell them that he had no home? No warmth of parents? When school friends invited him to a party, Karna would find an excuse for not going. If he were to go to friends' homes, he too would have to invite them home. But he had no home!

Karna worked very hard, and so it was natural that he would be ahead of the others. Karna had the full support of Dr. Bhagwati. Karna was not tardy in the work he did at the clinic, nor in his studies, nor in learning English. Dr. Bhagwati began to pay Karna Rs.200 a month. From that money, Karna paid fees, paid for his meals, and banked the small remainder. Karna's diligence paid off handsomely. Karna ranked among the top ten in the SSC board examinations. He got admission easily into a science college.

When he left the clinic to stay in a hostel, it was for Karna as traumatic an event as a bride leaving home after marriage. Although Dr. Bhagwati had not shown him the love of a father, he was the real sculptor of his life. Had Karna not met him, Karna's life would have taken an entirely different shape. The doctor expected nothing in return from mentoring him. His sole desire was to enable a potent seed to grow into a billowing tree. Seldom did Karna visit Dr. Bhagwati at his residence because seldom did the doctor remain at home. His real homes were his clinic and the hospitals he was attached to. The home was just an inn, useful only for sleeping at night. When he dropped off Karna at the hostel, the eyes of both were moist. Dr. Bhagwati put an arm around Karna's shoulder and said, "Do keep on coming." For the first time Karna embraced Dr. Bhagwati without feeling abashed.

Every Sunday Karna visited Dr. Bhagwati at his home and dined with him. He stayed the night, and left for college early on Monday morning. They were now developing a father-son relationship. The doctor was around 55. He was a widower, and had no children. This bright young man, with his amazing determination and effort, had found a place in his heart. Karna shared with him what he learned at college and also his independent views about it. Dr. Bhagwati recounted his unusual experiences.

With the help of Dr. Bhagwati, Karna got into a medical college. When for the first time a human corpse was to be dissected, compared to other students Karna could perform the task with the aplomb of a surgeon. Dr. Chhabaria, a friend of Dr. Bhagwati, specially phoned Dr. Bhagwati to tell him: "In all these years I have not yet seen a student with the surgical skills of this boy!"

Karna conducted experiments in his room. He would anaesthetize rabbits, and exchange their organs. He found out the circumstances in which such an exchange was possible. This was a breakthrough known as organ transplanting. In the course of time he fully succeeded in transplanting the heart, lungs, intestines, stomach, etc. in these animals. Now, having become a qualified surgeon, he was ready to try transplanting in humans. Slowly, like wind, his fame spread far and wide. He attended national and international conferences to speak on his technique and experiments.

Over twenty years had passed since he had last breathed the air of his native town. His memories of his town, parents, and life there had grown hazy. But one day, reading an invitation on his table, he felt dismantled, like a parcel of packets when the string holding it tight is loosened. A hospital was being inaugurated in his town and one Chhagan Parmar requested this 'famous surgeon' that the inauguration should be done at his hands! A mighty fight began between the desire to go and not go. What was the point of opening up the grave of distressing memories shoveled over with such an enormous effort? Yet Karna began to torture himself with the memories garnered from the folds of his past: of his town, friends, father and mother. It was like unconsciously scratching a painful pimple on the cheek to relish the pain. He felt an irresistible urge to go and find out whether his footprints still remained, or were completely obliterated in the hearts of his loved ones. 'But what if someone recognizes me?' Karna shuddered at the thought. 'What if I am recognized? Can you put an infant back into the womb after the umbilical cord is cut?'

He could not resolve this dilemma of going-not going. The next day was a Sunday and he decided to consult Dr. Bhagwati.

At the dining table 'father' and 'son' discussed the invitation. Both decided to travel together. Next Sunday they took their seats in an air-conditioned coach. The thought of the past intruding into the present and how he was to manage it weighed heavily on Karna's mind. Dr. Bhagwati was worried that he might lose a precious relationship once Karna met his natural parents.

The train stopped at Bharuch station. Both the doctors got into a taxi and told the driver to take them to Jambudia town. "Here's Jambudia—where shall I take the taxi?" The driver queried. Karna said, a bit faintly, "Take us to where the new hospital has come up." At the gates of the hospital Parmar and party welcomed them with much smiling and bowing. The stay was at Parmar's residence.

After the noon meal the guests sat on a swing in the house. The conversation drifted to the happenings in the town. Karna's tense breath gradually eased, as there was no mention of him or his family.

Practically the whole town turned up in the evening at the inaugural function. Karna cut the red ribbon tied to the hospital's gate. There was a big ovation. Everyone eyed Karna. Parmar, who was a trustee of the hospital, began his speech. He described how the hospital got built. The list of donors and the amounts donated were read out. Bored with the recitation of how the hospital would serve the town and what the town would have to do for the hospital, the town-folk started gossiping.

The audience became silent as soon as Karna got up to speak. Karna began by giving some idea about recent developments in medicine and surgery in other countries. The educated as well as the illiterate were greatly interested by his lucid description of the common ailments in the country, and how they could be tackled. He also suggested the steps the town-folk needed to take. He said, "Doctors are often not interested in people's health. Those doctors who follow the policy of keeping people sick so they can earn money are not fit to be called doctors." He folded his palms and sat down. People marveled at his erudition and simplicity.

After the garlanding ritual was over, Parmar escorted Karna and Dr. Bhagwati from the podium to a garden where they were to have refreshments with the leading lights of the town. Parmar started introducing each guest in turn. The first to be introduced was the town's chief priest. With the priest were his 20 years old son Kiran and 14 years old daughter Parvati. Karna greeted all three by folding his palms.

The cannon ball, restrained in the mind with such force, got fired. Karna felt like letting off a sky-piercing scream. 'I am Karna, your son who lived with you at one time. The one whose blood, flesh, and muscles are in me—even he has forgotten me!' The last bond of childhood snapped. That moment Karna became like a machine shut down by a power outage. He slumped, seeking the support of a chair.

"Do please come to our house for five minutes. The house's splendour vanished when the mother of these children died. If only you would have come four years earlier you would have diagnosed her malady. Who is that gentleman with you?"
"That . . . is my father. All the credit for my success goes to him."
"Doctorsaheb! This Kiran, the apple of my eye, is obedient like Rama! In these twenty years he has never once disobeyed me."

Karna looked at the fair, slightly bowed puppet standing adjacent to the priest, his shiny, oiled hair with a brahmin tuft fluttering in their midst, and vacant eyes. Kiran lowered his head, and out of becoming modesty at

the father's praise, started scratching the ground with his toe-nail. Karna forced his tongue to say something: "Kiranbhai, what do you do?"
"I accompany Father to perform religious ceremonies. Father is no longer able to carry the bag of gifted provisions. Now I go round the town's homes."
"Your father is lucky."

Questions and answers fought each other like wild beasts in Karna's mind:

'Have I no responsibility towards my old father?'
'It was your father who threw you out of the house and made you fatherless.'
'A wrong deed was done in a moment of anger. Perhaps later there was repentance.'
'As a son what will you be able to give to your father? Money? He does not need it. Love? Will you be able to give him love, like Kiran? To this enfeebled father the need is for a son who can carry a bag of provisions and obey his every command. When he threw you out also he wanted that kind of a son. Will you be able to be like that?'
'How can I become what I am not? And, what about my responsibility to my guardian father?'
'So what will you gain by revealing to a contented father that you are his discarded son? You will grieve his old heart. Leave quietly. Everyone's well-being is in that.'

Karna and Dr. Bhagwati sit in the taxi, say their goodbyes and depart. Karna leaves, his kin undisturbed like the well-arranged pieces of a chessboard.

THE GREAT GHOST HUNT

Our family tree is rather richly branched. In my grandparents' time if some wise chap tried to shout the family planning slogan 'We two and ours two', he would certainly have been beaten up. No sage had therefore provided my grandparents any such advice. And so my grandparents had six sons and three daughters—that is, I had five paternal uncles and three paternal aunts, all living together. In those times the slogan may have been 'We two and ours three', because each of my uncles and aunts had three children apiece, and they are all surviving. At our home we had a team larger than a cricket eleven, and we never had to depend on any outside kids to play any game.

Every summer vacation, our grandfather used to rent a bungalow at a resort and our entire family—tree, branches, foliage and all, migrated to the place and took root there. I have never seen my mother or other ladies of the house ever crowding into the kitchen, since we had two cooks. The principal cook was Ravishankar and his assistant was Manishankar. During the morning my grandparents used to be busy with prayers and browsing through newspapers. Their sons, daughters-in-law, daughters, and sons-in-law would roam the arterial paths of the place, and inhale fresh clean air worth its weight in gold. From the morning we kids would spend our time climbing trees, gathering wild berries like jambun and karamada, and painting our tongues dark purple. There would be frequent fights about the ownership of the fruit that was gathered. Divisions would take place, and choice abuses, though not unbecoming of our family's standing, would get freely pelted. Sulking never lasted long, for truce took place without reconciliation. No one liked to remain isolated for long.

Numerous games used to be played. In these, too, allegations of cheating were traded thick and fast. All the parents had clearly told us that while we were free to break each other's heads, we were never to take our complaints to the parents. And so, those unfairly treated would fume and say, "Who wants to play with you," break off from the game and start one of their own. All the mothers insisted that their kids must take an afternoon nap. So they led their children away to their respective rooms and bolted the rooms from inside. My mother would doze off, and I and my sisters would sleep next to her on each side. She, however, took the precaution to keep us pressed lightly to the bed with her feet. But generally we all succeeded in putting our respective mothers to sleep, and one by one the doors would stealthily open and we would slip out. All of us gathered in the garden for resuming our pranks.

After finishing dinner by about seven, the grownups played the card game of bezique. Even we joined in the game directly or indirectly. Accusations of cheating were made even by the grownups. Example: "The Queen of Spades was played earlier, but the son-in-law quietly retrieved it from the used up cards and used it again!" How often Grandpa, at the point of defeat, attributed the defeat to his unskilled partner, cheating by the opponents etc., threw down the cards, and did the male equivalent of a cross woman's lying down on the ground and throwing a tantrum. We had great fun watching these antics of the grownups, and we too would take sides and join in the fights. These games went on for a long time. In reality, however, we would be waiting for the cook Ravishankar to finish his chores and tell us a story.

Our grandfather had brought Ravishankar from a village when he was around ten. "When you came here you used to chop vegetables as though for feeding a goat! Had I not trained you so well, you would still have been a raw hand!" We would exult when Grandma scolded him thus. Any of us present would shake his or her head or index finger in approval, and mutter inside, "Oh! He deserves this!" We resented Ravishankar because he was the guardian of the kitchen and complained with a sweet tongue to Grandma if he caught us stealing stored goodies. This got us a chiding from her, and sometimes even a thrashing. When a favourite vegetable was cooked and we ate an extra couple of chapattis, he would immediately comment: "Oh! You are very hungry today, are you?" That taunt burnt us up, and then signaling to one another by winking, we would decide to teach the old man a lesson. Each tongue cast orders thick and fast: "Chapatti!" "Vegetable!" "Dal!" "Rice!" and so on. Poor Ravishankar would nearly collapse from exhaustion, trying to meet our rapid-fire orders. We felt glee seeing Ravishakar froth like a labouring horse!

During those vacation days, hearing a story was, for us, the peak of pleasure, and Ravishankar was as delighted telling us stories as he was gulping down laddoos[19]. And so, during the story telling interlude, the adversaries forgot their feuds and spontaneously got together for mutual enchantment. Ravishankar knew three kinds of stories: the doings of gods and goddesses recorded in ancient scriptures, of kings and queens, and of ghosts and vantaris[20]. We enjoyed all the three kinds, but I was especially fascinated by the ghost stories. Just as there are forms of chocolate, like éclair, toffee, and Toblorone, there are different sorts of ghosts—dakan, spirit, vantari, etc.

And then, there are differences even among ghosts. Dakan is a witch whose feet are turned backwards. Our face and feet are on the same side while hers are on the opposite side. Dakan looks in one direction, but walks in the reverse direction. From the front she would seem like any ordinary woman; but if she turned around you would only see a skeleton! She has no skin, flesh, blood, or muscle. Another sign of dakan is that she keeps a blazing stove around her neck. In his colourful, graphic, rustic language, Ravishankar's descriptions of dakan would turn nearby stubs of trees into witches on the move! And our terror-temperature would start climbing as we 'saw' her grab us in her sharp teeth and gulp us down!

Vantari is also a female ghost. Even today I can vividly recall one of his stories on my eye-screen: "One night I had gone to the outskirts of the village for answering the nature's call." *Now* one would immediately ask why he didn't go to the backyard or around the corner rather than all the way to the outskirts, and that too, at night! But at *that* time the question occurred to no one, and even if it did, it was not asked.

---

19 A sweetmeat especially favoured by brahmins

20 Nasty female spirits

"I had got practically to the outskirts when I saw a real beauty coming towards me. She was wearing red chaniya and choli and yellow odhani[21]. How ornaments shimmered on her body! She smiled at me and asked, 'Can I come . . . can I come?' If such a beauty asks 'Can I come with you?' then surely even a slack tongue would turn firm like a cucumber and say 'Yes'. I was about to say yes when Goddess Gayatri mentally forbade me."

"Why should Gayatridevi tell you to say no?" I had asked guilelessly.

"Do the sacred thread I wear and the evening prayers I recite twice daily have no value? Mother Gayatri warned me that this was a vantari. So, reluctantly I said no. At that a flame blazed, ankles jingled, there was raucous laughter like that of Krishna's demonic uncle Kamsa, darkness engulfed my sight, and I fainted. A passerby saw me and revived me, and got me home."

During many nights thereafter, I would hear 'Can I come, can I come'. I would tremble and perspire profusely. I would get sucked into a vortex of terror, but then my eyes would open and I would survive the nightmare. Ravishankar had told many such tales to us, and I remember every one of them. The fear would decimate my courage. My nightmares would squeeze me like all the eight feet of an octopus. And yet how I relished hearing those tales! I never had to sleep alone, since all of us kids used to sleep in one room. We felt very cozy—and safe—together. When we returned to Mumbai, Ravishankar would finish his chores, and saunter off to the Chowpatty beach to be with his chums. We, too, would be busy with homework and therefore would have little time for hearing stories. And so, it was during the summer vacation that we gorged ourselves on those stories.

Years rolled by. Yet the fascination with ghost stories and the constant fear of ghosts continued. One day I came across a thick volume on ghosts. I read it through with bated breath. In it was a story about a hospital where the author claimed to have seen a spirit with his own eyes. The hospital is a living grave. Innumerable unfulfilled desires reverberate around from pangs of suffering. For a few moments I was convinced that if there are ghosts, they would certainly reside in the hospital. Though

21 Chaniya is a skirt, choli a blouse, and odhani a loose garment for the female torso

these moments passed, they instilled a fear in me that haunted me in the times to come.

Once I suddenly had a pain in my stomach. School to home was about a ten-minute walk. Normally the distance would pass almost unconsciously. But that day the aching stomach made me count every step. On getting home I collapsed on a bed. I slept on my back, on my stomach, on one side, then the other. But the pain remained excruciating. Mother came. The doctor was called. He pressed my stomach at different places, and based on the variation in my squeals, he diagnosed: "Looks like appendicitis." Next day, X-rays were taken and examined, and it was announced that the appendix was inflamed and if this got worse I might depart at age 16! I was therefore shifted to a hospital. The pain in my abdomen was unbearable, but the overwhelming agony of encountering ghosts in the hospital dampened my abdominal pain.

When patients died in the hospital, they were removed to the backyard. My room was almost exactly above this litter of corpses. The daily wailing of near and dear ones made me almost forget that I was alive. Often I visualized my relatives weeping after me. Morning and evening I could pass in reading and talking to my visitors. But during every waking moment at night the fear of ghosts went on a rampage within me. Each of the fifteen nights I spent in the hospital turned into my cortege. Fear of running into a ghost kept kneading my brain.

I used to look with suspicion at every unfamiliar nurse, sweeper, ward boy, or doctor. At night nurses would not let one sleep in peace. They would grasp your hand with a jerk to examine your pulse, or to raise your arm and insert a thermometer in your armpit. Their starched apparel was matched by their starchy behaviour. Even laughter seemed to have been rinsed in starch, since their lips were stuck together stiffly so that their teeth were never visible. Once, a nurse dropped in at night. I had not seen her before. A tremor shot through me.

Mother was sleeping on a cot at the other end of my room. I felt like getting up and clinging to her. But the stitches were still there. And so I lay on the bed like a petrified doll. I tried to grasp the nurse's arm, saying, "Are you a ghost or a real nurse?" She left the room. Did she, because she was a ghost? But after this incident my fear declined rather than increased.

If she was truly a ghost then I had nothing to fear since she was not able to cause me any harm. And I had enough courage to hold her hand. So, I was after all, not as cowardly as I thought.

Ravishankar used to say that ghosts are mightily afraid of the Gayatri chant. The ghost bursts into a flame as soon as it hears the Gayatri mantra. I had learnt the Gayatri mantra; but I had not yet tried it out on a ghost. Perhaps I could have tested out the power of the mantra had I recited Gayatri when that nurse came inside for taking my pulse. Once again a nurse came into my room. I immediately began to recite Gayatri. I kept reciting Gayatri. She gave me an injection and left. She did not burst into flames. I therefore decided that she was a genuine nurse.

I started walking the day my stitches were removed. At midnight I started loitering about in the corridor outside my room. I had decided to eradicate my fear. I stood near a window. In the verandah of the ground floor a man was moving about in a wheel chair. From the thigh to the heel his feet were bandaged. His face looked charred. Why would he be afoot so late at night? May be for the same reason as myself! I collected all my wits, recited the Gayatri mantra, and called out loudly, "Sir, what has happened to you?" My fear subsided a little as I spoke. Surprised, he looked up at the first floor, and said in a weak voice, "Both my legs were shot. Just a few days back I was operated to remove the bullets. I feel a little better today so I am moving about." I wandered around for a couple of hours, looked outside the window, talked to anyone I chanced to see. After two hours I became light as the wings of a butterfly and fluttered off to slumber.

The very next day I was allowed to go home. I felt as if someone had transported me from a white, snowy desert to a landscape of multi-coloured fountains. At home, colours flamed everywhere—on curtains, sofa covers, wall paintings, rugs. How I had pined in the hospital for even a smudge of paint!

I remained at home for 8-10 days after returning from the hospital. Then the Diwali holidays came and I went off to my mother's grandmother's home in Porbandar. My mother's mother had died in childbirth, so 'Nanima' had raised my mother. At one time Nanima was very wealthy. Her husband had been a highly respected merchant who had died twenty years back. Nanima was all of hundred years old. But her ears and limbs were still so green! Her sight had dimmed and she stooped a little, but her mind was still strong like hardwood. She lived all alone in a huge mansion. Adjacent were the servants' quarters, so she could summon servants with a shout. One night I asked Nanima: "Nanima! Are you afraid of anything?"

"I am not afraid of anything. What fear can I have when I am not afraid of dying? But you tell me, what are you afraid of?"
"I am afraid of ghosts", I said with embarrassment.
"We know nothing about ghosts. This ignorance is the basis of our fear. I used to be afraid when I was your age. When I grew a little older, I hardened my resolve to overcome it and went at night to the crematorium—the crematorium behind this mansion. I sat there all night. When I returned next morning your great grandfather gave me a slap so hard that there was a red welt on my cheek! But from that day I was totally rid off the fear of ghosts."
"Nanima, you saw nothing in the crematorium?"
"I did get terrorized frequently by the shadows of trees as they moved about in the breeze. But I felt okay when I threw the light of my battery at them. I was mortified that day by the calls of chibris[22]. The ti-n-ti-n-ti-n sound was like death's whistling. When there was movement in piles of dried leaves around me I thought I heard the footfalls of someone coming after me. Thank God I had a powerful battery. Otherwise, if I had not seen what actually was there, I would surely have seen many ghosts! I spent the whole night in the grip of fear. When I was small, my servants used to tell many ghost stories, and my fear had got ingrained then."
"Nanima, can I go to the crematorium?"
"You are too young to go alone, but I will send Hari with you."

Nanima shouted for Hari. Hearing her whip-like summons at eleven at night he jumped to his feet and shuffled to Nanima in bewilderment. He stared vacantly at Nanima when she ordered him to take me to the crematorium. Then he started exhaling puffs of incoherent, guttural sounds. He made innumerable excuses for not going, and finally succeeded.

---

22 A small owl-like bird

Nanima angrily seized a walking stick to walk with me to the crematorium. I held a torch and a mat in my hands. In a little while we got to the center of the crematorium. The last puffs of smoke were emanating from a funeral pyre. Two cremators were fast asleep on their charpoys. A little distance away was a huge peepal[23] tree. There was a platform around the tree. I spread the mat on it. Nanima comfortably seated herself on it. "Now run off for a round of the crematorium", Nanima directed, and my eyelashes fluttered with fright. "You won't be able to see any ghosts if you keep the battery lit. Keep it off and light it only when you see a ghost", Nanima advised.

The grounds of the crematorium were about two acres in extent. To measure my fear-score I deliberately moved far away from Nanima. How many shadows appeared like ghosts to me! But as soon as light fell on them, the twigs on the trees, the leaves, and the rags fluttering from branches guffawed at my cowardice. I could roam around because of the thread tying me to Nanima; otherwise I could not have gone to the crematorium alone. I wandered around for nearly half an hour. Then I returned and sat by Nanima.

Nanima suddenly remembered my mother's mischief when she was small. One day my mother crept into a cupboard. Nanima could not find her anywhere. After searching everywhere, she informed the police. Nanima was slumped on a cot. Then she heard a faint sound of someone crying. She sat bolt upright. "The sound was from the cupboard . . .", she exclaimed, and then she burst out laughing. I was in stitches and my laughter kept rolling on and on, like a can tumbling down a rough incline. One of the cremators heard our laughter. He sat up with a convulsion. He screamed when he saw us. We were startled. The other fellow also leaped out of his bed. Quickly Nanima shouted, "I am Harkorba. This daughter wanted to see a crematorium, so I brought her over." Jagiyo and Damlo felt a bit reassured. "Mother, is crematorium a place for taking a walk? And should anyone come here at this time of night?" Damlo spat out his grievance.
"My daughter insisted on seeing the crematorium at night, and so I brought her over."
"Don't ghosts bother you here?" I feared the answer.

23 Ghosts are believed to reside on this tree

"We have stayed several nights here, but we haven't seen anything. But I could have died hearing your laughter!" There was still a tremor in Damlo's voice.

I got close to the cremators, and asked, "You have never seen any ghost, witch, vantari, or meladi in the crematorium?" Both shook their heads.
"We are leaving. Now go back to sleep."
"Not now! Sleep has vanished." Damlo took out his pipe and began to stuff tobacco into it, and Jagiyo began to talk about the local exorcist.

"Yesterday the exorcist thrashed Kanku Parjapati with his slippers. He said a vantari had possessed her."
"Poor woman! Got beaten up for no reason. Bah! What ghosts? See! Only a little while back Jagiyo practically fainted from our laughter. Had I not identified myself as Harkorba, then by morning he would have got a burning fever, and you would have taken him to the exorcist to get rid off the ghost! Then you would have gone round yelling everywhere that there is a ghost in the crematorium!"

Both felt abashed and looked down. We bade goodbye and returned home. I felt as if my fear had trickled away through a sieve and was out of me. In a surge of affection, I twined my thin arms around Nanima. It was as if Nanima had jerked the infantile habit of sucking out of me. I stayed with Nanima for a fortnight; but I kept feeling that I was staying with a friend. She was effusive. But she also had the gumption and intelligence of a sage. Nanima was such a strong person! So I was astonished to see tears in her eyes when I left for Mumbai. It was like a lioness weeping. Nanima took my head in her hands and kissed it so many times! These were her last kisses.

When I returned to Mumbai the exams were only a few days away. We all three sisters slept together in a room; but today there were several special guests—two girl friends of each of my two sisters. My uncle had expired about four months back. At night I decided to study in the empty room. For two-three hours I was engrossed in reading. Then my eyes fell upon my uncle's photo framed on a wall. I recalled vividly each phase of his death. Clouds of fear again darkened my mind. I was reading in the chair I had kept near a window. Suddenly a long tooth fell on me. I got so frightened that leaving the tooth where it was I fled to my room, spread a mat on the floor and took refuge in the crowded midst of my sisters and their friends. I once again vowed to myself—a vow taken many times before—that I would triumph over my fear.

The next day in the daylight I was more courageous. I went to the uncle's room and examined the tooth carefully. How did it fall all of a sudden on me? For more light I moved the curtain aside to open the window. Immediately a small bone fell on me. When I examined the curtain on both sides I found a sticky substance on one side. A crow must have deposited this substance while feeding on flesh. The crow must have left the tooth stuck to the curtain. This possibility got engraved on my mind, and after that the fear evaporated. The next two days I slept alone in the uncle's room. However, I did keep the light on . . . !

When I was around eleven, Ravishankar retired from our service and went to live in Rajota, his village near Idar, in North Gujarat. He had got his son admitted for a B.A. in Mumbai and this boy had got the job of a clerk in an office with my father's help. Ravishankar and his wife Dhuliben came to Mumbai to live with their son. They had aged, and their eyes, ears, teeth had deteriorated. So, when they were unable to look after each other, they went for support to their son and daughter-in-law. In due course Ravishankar and Dhuliben came to meet us. As soon as I saw them I became impatient to clear my mind about the ghost stories that had plagued my mind and kept the lava of fear boiling within me.

"How are you Ravishankar Bhatt, do you remember me?"
"Of course! You are Avani. You must think that marbles have replaced the irises of my eyes."

I boldly cut in during the pleasantries: "Those stories about witches and vantaris you used to tell us when we were small—were they true stories, or . . . ?"
"Which story?" He asked, rummaging into his memory. I re-told two or three in his own words.

"Silly girl! All those were just tales. Do you think I have met any witch or vantari?"
"You have never seen a ghost?" I was incredulous.

"People from our village talk a lot about their powers. They say that our exorcist chases off ghosts and spirits with incantations. But I have never seen anything with my own eyes", Ravishankar said, laughing toothlessly.

Inside, I rained abuses on him. The man who planted ghosts in my mind had no knowledge of their existence!

The next day I was reading a newspaper. I chanced to see a boldly printed headline: 'A Scooter Rider's Experience of a Spirit'. I read the story breathlessly. 'On the Princess Street—Marine Drive flyover, Mr Bomi Daruwala was riding his scooter at night the other day. The scooter stalled midway. It failed to start despite all efforts. Bomibhai heard a sound. He heard a hoarse laughter. Bomibhai looked around, but saw no one. Suddenly a skull fell at his feet. He felt an inhuman, cold touch. He fainted.'

I called the office of 'Mumbai Samachar' and asked who had written this story. On the phone it turned into the game of asking the cat to get the dog. So I personally went to the newspaper's office. The editor pointed out the desk of the person who had reported this story. He in turn told me that a neighbour of his neighbour who was Bomibhai's friend had told him the story. He had personally not met Bomibhai. I waited there until the office closed. Despite the intense displeasure of Jeevabhai—the reporter—I accompanied him home and met his neighbour. The neighbour said, "A friend of my neighbour had said that Bomibhai was his neighbour's friend's brother—in-law's friend." Despite the disapproval of my parents, I had bunked classes for three days; but the Bomibhai I finally tracked down said, "Certainly not, that chap must be some other Bomi. I have not met any ghost or spirit. By the way who gave you this stupid and baseless story?" Bomibhai boiled when he heard it was Mumbai Samachar, and the very next day he set off for its office to turn the journalist's brain into roiled curd!

I enrolled for a Master's degree in psychology. Freud, the pre-eminent psychologist of the 20th century, fascinated me. I read a lot on his technique of psychoanalysis, and also got some training from an expert. According to Freud, the roots of many physical illnesses lie in mental illness. Our fear of examinations may get converted into fever, boredom at work into headache, mother's neglect of the child to child falling sick to get attention. I had studied all these cursorily during my studies for the Bachelor's degree. But I had not grasped their essence or significance fully. I had remained at the ABC level; but now I felt that through the alphabet of psychology I could interpret the human cosmos. It was like crossing the seven seas of psychology and finding a magical key that opened up for view the entire internal landscape. I relished my studies so much that I was barely conscious of completing my requirements for the degree.

I met a young man, and we fell in love. This resulted in marriage. My husband was a doctor. He was highly principled and service minded. He decided to go to a village of Gujarat and serve its people. I joined him with great enthusiasm.

Gilodiya was a village of 5000 souls. Thakors, kanabis, and harijans were the main communities. It was easy to identify to which community member a house belonged by looking at its structure, internal arrangements, and the number, shape and shine of brass vessels. One day, while sauntering, I chanced to see a noisy crowd. Elbowing people aside I got to the center of the crowd. A woman was rolling on the ground. Her ragged, disheveled hair were smeared with dust. She was screaming horribly. The surrounding black heads were humming like honeybees. One man was kicking her. I shouted above the din: "Why are you beating the poor woman?" The man looked at me with disdain, as if I was a dumb person, and said, "Don't you see that a vantari has possessed her?"

I rushed to the police station and requested the chief to accompany me. As soon as we reached the place the chief said harshly, "I am not foolish enough to intervene. She may devour me too." He left without looking at me. Had I been one of the villagers, I too might have got a thrashing. But I was from the city and educated, so they kept respect by ignoring my existence and continuing their work. I was horrified. Couldn't say anything, couldn't bear this either! The beating continued while the woman was dragged to her house. I too was pushed along in the current. An exorcist was called. He brought along an incense pot. He wore on his head a red head-dress. He was dressed in a white shirt and dhoti. The woman was lying on the ground half dead. The exorcist spread smoke around her from the incense pot and started incanting magic spells. He began to sway his head from side to side and shouted: "Speak up! Who are you, where have you come from?" The question was repeated three-four

times. The woman's lips moved a little and then grew still. "I will burn you if you don't speak up. Tell me! Who are you?" The exorcist hissed in anger. He asked an aged woman to heat a rod. She enthusiastically made a rod red hot and gave it to the exorcist. The exorcist pressed it into the poor woman's palm. Her scream rent the sky. Those present relished the juicy show. My determination turned to dust. I ran for solace to my husband. My sobs flowed like a torrent. Shripad kept caressing my head and asking, "What happened?" But my speech was ground into dust. After calming down a little I recounted the episode. I said, "Seeing this violence and keeping quiet is also an offence."
"Avani! We have only recently come here. We will create only enmity if we tell them that their belief is wrong".

Next day I went to see the woman. She lay curled in a heap on the floor like some unwanted thing. Her family members pushed her aside with their feet in bestial glee, as they passed her by. I was shocked by this demon in man. My confidence in mankind began to evaporate into thin air. I felt dubious even about myself. My eyes began to fear peering inside myself.

I became friendly with the woman's neighbours. I learned from one of them the details of her family. Her name was Manchhi. Her husband hated her. He was cruel and a drunkard. Daily he would get drunk on lattha[24] and beat up Manchhi. The mother-in-law would instigate her son to beat her some more with a stick. The husband drank away one by one all of Manchhi's ornaments. The mother-in-law did not give her even enough to eat. As if they had decided to get rid off her, daily the mother-in-law would tell her, "Why don't you die so that we are rid off you."

Four months earlier Manchhi had borne a daughter. The infant had six fingers on each hand. The exorcist cast her horoscope and pronounced her inauspicious. Once, Manchhi had kept the baby on the verandah while she cooked inside. When she came out, there was no daughter! Lord knows what happened to her. The husband and the mother-in-law celebrated the disappearance by eating lapsi[25]. From that day on Manchhi

---

24 A locally brewed alcoholic drink
25 A sweet generally eaten on auspicious occasions

became practically crazed. The exorcist could not rid Manchhi's madness by incantations, charmed strings, or burns.

Manchhi's situation was going from bad to worse. The exorcist declared that this woman's possession was so stubborn that it would not rest until the life was taken.

One day, Manchhi's husband deposited Manchhi on our verandah. "I don't want this vantari. You keep her if you want to." I could not bear to abandon Manchhi. She stayed on at our place. I showered affection on her. I gave her small chores to keep her occupied. Initially she would suddenly scream and I would get torn apart by fear for her. But in two months there was certainly some improvement. She stopped screaming and rolling on the ground. But she was mute like a snake hibernating in winter. However, the agony inside her sometimes leaped out of the eyes.

About that time I gave birth to a son. I was, of course, ecstatic. But Manchhi was even more thrilled. It was as if spring had sprouted on her face. My Tapas became the cure for her disease. My home became hers, too.

These days everyone admires her comeliness when she goes out for household shopping. Manchhi warmly welcomes Shripad's patients, as well as mine with phobias similar to Manchhi's. She serves them chilled water and courage: "Since you have come here, you will certainly be cured."

It is Manchhi who looks after, feeds, puts to sleep, and fondles my Tapas. I have given her all the freedoms. But I have warned her sternly about one matter: "Never tell Tapas a ghost story!"

KALIYO

Eleven years old Shyamli and her mother Saroj are on the swing in their garden, slowly swaying back and forth. The mother is at one end of the swing and the daughter, her head in the mother's lap, is stretched out on the swing. Shyamli's abundant long, untied hair float lazily in the breeze, like the monsoon's undulating clouds.

The mother and the daughter are tired from hard work—there has been no servant during the past month. Shyamli is unusually sensitive. Were someone to insult or speak roughly to her, she would cave inwards into an aching ball.

Shyamli is very fond of stories. Once she commences reading a story, she forgets everything, even eating. And sometimes she remembers to go to the toilet only after her groin begins to rebel. Her second passion is singing. If she is not talking or reading, Shyamli is singing. Her mother's voice, too, is melodious and trained. It can glide effortlessly in three octaves.

While on the swing, Shyamli remembered a jhoola (swing) composition. "Ma, please sing that song 'Slowly rock the swing, Nandlal'". Shyamli's eyes begin to droop, consciousness dissolving in the mother's lilt. But remembering that she had yet to say good night to Pappa, she goes to his room with drowsy eyes. Dad's day begins when Shyamli's ends—he works late into the night. Shyamli's father is an architect. Right now he is engrossed in making a blueprint for a building, "Pappa you put me to sleep and tell me a story—then I will return this pen", saying she seizes the sketch pen in her father's hand. Shyamli pulls her dad's hand and drags him to her bed in the living room. Shyamli stretches out on the mattress, and caressing Shyamli's silken hair, the father starts the story of the Egyptian pharaoh Khufu (Cheops). He is talking about the majestic pyramid constructed by him when Shyamli interrupts him with a flurry of questions:

"Pappa! Who first conceived the shape of the pyramid? The pharaoh, or some great architect?"
"Must be some super-bright architect like me."
"Pappa! No 'must be.' Do you know who he was?"
"Yes, his name was 'Bok.' But the first pyramid was designed by an architect named 'Imhotep'."
"Can you build a pyramid?"
"May be."
"How did that shape enter his head, five thousand years back?"
"Shyamli! I don't' know."
"In that desert, Pappa, from where did they get such huge stones? Were there cranes then to lift stones?"
"People then were not feathers like you that they would fly away with a puff of breath! Maybe a team of hefty dozen fellows pulled each massive 25 ton stone onto a wooden sledge, and dragged it for miles."
"Pappa! Were these men labourers?"
"No, Shyamli. They were slaves. A hundred thousand slaves worked to build the Gizeh Pyramid."
"Pappa! Would the pharaoh beat a slave who did not work properly?"
"So many slaves died in the construction of the pyramid! The slave-owner has total authority over the body, mind, and life of his slaves. That is why they are called slaves. If you do not do work properly, then I can't beat you; not even scold you!"
"Pyramid was more a heap of the corpses of slaves than the pharaoh's grave, isn't it? Pappa! The pharaoh should be called a man-eater!"

Pappa felt that he was a fool to start the tale of the pyramid. He tried to divert her mind. "Shyamli, I am building a theatre whose stage can revolve."
"Pappa! Don't divert my attention . . . that pharaoh . . ."

Shyamli was a bureau of unlimited questions. The father was finally fed up. He got up, shut off the light, and ordered Shyamli to go to sleep!

Twice during the night Shyamli got up, crying and screaming "Don't beat him . . . don't beat him!" The mother gently stroked her back and put her back to sleep.

The next day was a Sunday, and due to the night's disturbed sleep, Shyamli got up late. While sitting in the bed and thinking of the helplessness of slaves, she saw a short boy of about her age dusting the sofa with a cloth. Shyamli ran to her mother to ask about this stranger.

"Our neighbour Rambhaben has sent him, saying that this boy is known to her servant, and has just come from the village. She has said plainly that he should be kept if his work is satisfactory, and if not, he should be dispensed with. The pay is sixty rupees a month. His duties in the morning are sweeping, scrubbing, laundry, and dishes; dishes again in the afternoon. That's his work. What a relief Shyamli! We are now free from servitude."
"Ma! Would you make me do so much work? Would his mother have made him do so much work?"
"Shyamli! He has come to work on his own—I have not fetched him from his home . . . he must have come because his mother sent him, don't you think?"

Mother said this, but she felt a pang for saying such insensitive words. She kissed Shyamli's head again and again, possibly to alleviate the sting in her heart.

"Shyamli! If he gets tired, we will help him a little."
"Only a little, yes?" Shyamli burst out laughing.

Shyamli went to this new servant and asked lightly, "What is you name?"
"Kaliyo", he replied, eyes lowered.
"You are not dark, so why did your mother name you 'Kaliyo'?" He smiled, still with lowered eyes.
"What village are you from?"
"Dungarpur."
"You have never been to a city before?"
He shook his head.
"If you do not know anything about your work, don't be afraid to ask. And if you feel tired, don't hesitate to tell my mother."

Kaliyo raised his head as if confused, narrowed his eyes, and wrinkled his forehead. Shyamli laughed with affection. Engrossed in reading a storybook, Shyamli quite forgot Kaliyo for an hour or so.

Remembering him, she immediately ran to where Kaliyo was squeezing the water out of soaked clothes. Mother shouted, "Wring the clothes properly. See that no water remains." But his hands were too small to hold sodden clothes properly. Shyamli said, "You hold one end and I'll hold the other—this way, wringing them will be easier." The two together wrung the clothes dry.

Kaliyo thanked her with his eyes.

Shyamli took out four biscuits from a jar. She kept two and extended her hand to give the other two to Kaliyo. Kaliyo did not extend his hand. "Take! If you work hard, won't you get hungry? Take, no one will scold you!" Slowly Kaliyo extended his hand, took the biscuits and began to eat in a corner.

Mother saw this, but said nothing in front of Kaliyo. After he had gone, she told Shyamli, "If you form bad habits like this, he will commit theft when he is not given snacks."
"Ma! Won't he feel like committing a theft because he is not given food? What would be wrong if we give a small portion of our snacks to him? On the day we don't have snacks, he too will not get any."

Mother saw the force of the logic partially but also felt annoyed. Shyamli's school timings were 7.30 a.m. to 11.30 a.m. The next day she got up early, got ready, and went to the school as usual. As soon as Kaliyo came he went round the rooms looking for Shyamli. He felt depressed at not finding her. That day the work weighed heavily on his shoulders.

Shyamli opened the door that afternoon when Kaliyo came to clean the vessels. Happiness surged over his face. Standing near the sink he started cleaning the vessels, and sitting on the floor, Shyamli began to converse with him.

"Kaliyo! How many brothers do you have?" Kaliyo indicated five with his fingers.

"Vow! So many! How many sisters?"
His thumb moved to signify none.
"Are you the youngest?"
"The oldest!"

Kaliyo was a villager, and so both found it difficult to understand what the other was saying. Thus there were confusions; but both made the effort to resolve them.

Everyday, when Kaliyo came for his afternoon duties at 2 p.m., Shyamli would be ready with her questions. In just a few weeks Shyamli learnt a lot about Kaliyo. Kaliyo's father was a farmer. He had only a little land, and with drought during the past three years, how was he to feed so many mouths? The three eldest sons were sent off to other towns. Cultivation was assigned to his wife and eight year old twin sons. The father also took a job at some other place to pay off debts. Shyamli trembled at the thought—"Broken home! How family members have got scattered—all for want of money . . . !"

Many questions arose also in Kaliyo's mind; but they were still misty—an elephant one moment, a swan another. And little Kaliyo would get confused trying to voice these hazy questions. Shyamli would gently draw out these hazy questions like an expert spinner of yarn. "Kaliyo, this is what you think, isn't it?" Kaliyo would respond with "Yes" or "No". He began to take forward mental steps, holding on to Shyamli's thinking fingers.

Sometimes Shyamli used to read out a story to Kaliyo, and sometimes recount to him in detail what happened at school—the mischief of some of the tailless monkeys of the class, the temperament of the class teacher, how he dressed, how he taught, and so forth. Sometimes she shared with him what she learnt in different subjects. Kaliyo used to listen to her without batting an eyelid. Those days of the hesitant first steps at getting acquainted stretched into two years of bonding.

Now Kaliyo could question Shyamli without fear, and share his concerns as effortlessly as a branch's swaying in the breeze. Kaliyo did not talk about history/geography like Shyamli, but he could describe quite expertly how seeds are planted, how grain is harvested, the harvesting seasons, how to make a hut of mud and cow dung, how to help a cow bellowing in pain to deliver her calf quickly. Shyamli would get impressed by this 'scholar.' The newspapers might go wrong in predicting when it would rain; but not Kaliyo, who could make correct predictions on the basis of the direction from which dark clouds came and how the wind blew at the time. During the monsoon she used to check with Kaliyo before going to school—"Kaliyo! Shall I take the umbrella today?" Rain would not fall if Kaliyo had firmly said no. Shyamli found her bookish knowledge dull, and felt that before Kaliyo's experience-based knowledge all her tomes were worthless.

Shyamli stood out as entirely different in her dialogues with her schoolmates as well as with neighbourhood girl friends. The parents often wondered how such a mature intelligence could reside in a thirteen years old person.

Consider what happened just two days earlier. Shyamli had borrowed a storybook from Surabhi, daughter of their neighbour Revaben. Inside the book, Shyamli found a love letter of Surabhi addressed to the film star Amitabh Bachhan. Shyamli laughed and laughed on reading it. She caught hold of Surabhi's hand and pulling her along to the swing in her garden said, "Silly girl, how can you write such a letter? How did you fall in love with Amitabh? Just by seeing films? You must have been blinded by his acting style; otherwise how could you love a person you do not know at all?"

Surabhi stared dumbly at Shyamli. She did not seem to comprehend.

The mother, listening to this dialogue from the living room window, was pleased as punch at the daughter's logic and maturity.

The mother began to worry about the friendship of Shyamli and Kaliyo just about the time Shyamli was to turn thirteen, especially about Kaliyo's coming between 2 p.m. and 3 p.m. when the mother was snoozing. So Kaliyo's time was changed to 1 p.m. The mother began to hover around Shyamli to keep an eye on her.

Today is Shyamli's fourteenth birthday. Since there was a big celebration the previous year, the mother decided not to invite friends this time. She had made puranpoli[26] for lunch. Shyamli thought that there was not enough puran for Kaliyo, so she ate two puranpolis and kept one aside for him. The mother asked the reason for keeping one aside. Shyamli answered truthfully without any hesitation. The mother was annoyed, but said nothing, for in her heart she was happy that her child had the purity of heart that she did not possess.

When Kaliyo came in the afternoon, Shyamli was embroidering a handkerchief in the living room. "Shyamli! Close your eyes—I have brought something for you. Come on! Extend your hand!"

Kaliyo turned out both his pockets and filled both palms of Shyamli with 'badams'—the red fruit of almonds. Even with eyes shut Shyamli recognized the fruit. Shyness and pleasure suffused her face with many contrasting hues. Quickly opening her eyes, Shyamli looked tenderly at Kaliyo and said, "Now you close your eyes and open your mouth!" Shyamli ran to the kitchen to fetch the puranpoli, and put a piece in his mouth—"Tell me, what is it?"

The mother came there at that very moment. She froze in shock. The mother scolded, not verbally, but with the reddening of her skin and the anger in the eyes. The mother erupted as soon as Kaliyo finished his work and left:

"You have turned fourteen and still you do not know how to behave with a male? If you do this again then . . ."

Cutting off the sentence, Shyamli exploded like the seed of corn that are being roasted on fire, "Ma! You are just like a frog in a well. What did I do to Kaliyo? Did I embrace him? Kiss him? You are attacking me just because I put a morsel of puranpoli in his mouth! You are afraid, aren't you, that if this goes on I will fall in love with Kaliyo—then marry him against your wishes—and you will be pilloried in society—everyone will exclaim, 'What, Sarojben's daughter married a servant?!' Nothing of the kind is going to happen."

---

26 Chapatti stuffed with a sweetmeat called 'puran'

The mother stared wide-eyed at the daughter, stunned by her verbal blows. Shyamli's tongue ran fast, like a car speeding on a highway.

"Kaliyo is my friend and I am not going to break his friendship because of your fear, and there is absolutely no need for you to pull him up."

Realizing that she need not have been so aggressive, Shyamli calmed down. The flames on her cheeks subsided. Embracing her mother, she whispered softly in her ears, "Ma! I am sorry! Ma, you are worrying unnecessarily. You will not find such a sensible daughter like me even if you go round the whole world with a searchlight! I will study a lot. I will become an archaeologist, and the one I marry will be so bright that you will have to shut your eyes!"

The mother continued to stare at her daughter. Then she hugged her tight in a paroxysm of affection.

"Ma, will Kaliyo be consigned for life to the menial world of cleaning vessels and places? He can do something more intelligent. Ma, shouldn't we help him to rise in life?"

Saroj continued to stare. Shyamli's face dissolved in her eyes. Her mother's face arose instead.

Despite Saroj's father's opposition, Saroj's mother used to send Ravji, a boy-servant, to night school. The dinner used to be over by 7.30 pm to enable Ravji to reach school in time. Sometimes, father used to shout in anger, "I have compulsorily to get hungry to suit Ravji!" Sometimes, at the peak of his rage, vessels used to be flung. Mother used to plead with father to calm down. What an outpouring of tears there was in mother's eyes when Ravji got a job in a bank due to the education he had got!

This remembrance, lasting just a few moments, transformed Saroj's attitude towards Kaliyo.

After that day, Kaliyo could lean on three shoulders for rising in life. It was Thursday. When Kaliyo came in the afternoon, Shyamli laughed and said, "Hello Mr. Kalidas! How are you?" Not knowing whether to turn angry or to laugh this away, Kaliyo stared suspiciously at Shyamli.

"You wanted so much to study like me, isn't it? Ma has said that she will pay for your fees. See now! Your Thursday[27] has become fruitful."
"Really?" The overwhelmed mind could say no more.
"You don't think so?"
"But if I start school at this age when will I finish it? And then work . . . ?"
"O my sixty years old friend! You will complete your studies at eighty!"
"Wouldn't I look over-aged in the class? I would have to start only from the fifth standard. In Dungarpur I had studied up to the fourth standard. Suppose you have to start studying now and sit with an eleven years old girl?"
"Look! You can take the 8 pm to 10 pm SSC[28] private coaching classes. There will be youngsters there of your age or older. Right now it is September. You study with me from September to June. See, you will not find geography, history, physiology and hygiene at all difficult because every day for the past three years I have been explaining to you what I learnt at school. In the remaining eight-nine months let us study together the ninth standard materials. You do not opt for English and mathematics. Instead you elect carpentry, typing or something like that."
"Shyamli! If my parents were educated and well-to-do like yours, you would not have mocked me."
"O my brother! I am not mocking you. Nowadays for SSC you have to select only six subjects out of so many!"
"I can't pass", Kaliyo said, shaking his head like a pendulum.
"Why should you fail if you work hard? You are not dumb like Revaben's Umesh. Why are you hammering your courage down? I will not allow you to scrub vessels, and nor will I allow you to turn into a bullock of an office peon."

Kaliyo saw his sunrise in Shyamli's transparent eyes.

Out of the blue, there was a telegram from Kaliyo's home that his mother was very ill and he should come immediately. Normally Kaliyo would go

27 An auspicious day among Hindus
28 Secondary School Certificate

home during Holi[29], and all his five brothers would also congregate. They would get very boisterous. Their childhood companions also would take leave and gather into the village. Kaliyo would slip into childhood and totally forget his job. But now there certainly were fights about cleanliness and order at home. The parents and brothers used to get irritated, saying "What a great money-bag we see here!" Kaliyo had absorbed the culture of Shyamli's house. His personality had acquired a special sheen, as if from coatings of gold leaf.

He reached his village in a panic. He crossed his courtyard breathlessly. The mother was winnowing grain, energetic as a mare. Kaliyo was shocked. Explaining, the mother said, "We had to take recourse to the ruse of my sickness, as otherwise you would not have come for your marriage. We have fixed your marriage with Laxmi, the daughter of Danaji Sagara, who owns a brick-and-mortar house."
Ma! I will not marry."
"This is a question of our reputation. We have given our promise. The marriage is next week. You can leave after that."

Kaliyo remained silent. But next day he took the 4 am bus and pressed the bell of Shyamli's house in the afternoon. Shyamli opened the door.

"Kaliyo . . . ! You didn't go?"
"My mother lied to get me married. I did not want my life to be scuttled!"

During the previous five years, he had firmed up ideas about marriage after coming into contact with many people. He wanted to marry someone who would be a life partner. He had no home still, nor the ability to look after a wife. He did not want to cast his hapless children on the street, as his parents had to, because they could not afford to nurture them properly. In these circumstances, marriage was out of the question.

After careful thought and after taking into account his capabilities and inclinations, he decided on getting further education in farming. Quite possibly, he might not have come to this conclusion without the aid of

29 A festival of colours

Shyamli's insights. But now the bud of volition had sprouted on Kaliyo's branch, and Kaliyo did what it commanded.

Kaliyo was obsessed with wanting to learn scientific farming, and how to grow a treasure of golden corn on little land. Shyamli's dad used his influence to get Kaliyo admitted to Anand's Institute of Farming and Dairying. The family took Kaliyo in the car to Anand, as if to see off a family member. The moment of their parting came. Tears dripped from Saroj's eyes; they turned back after stopping at Sureshbhai's eyelids; and Shyamli, drowning her eyes in a flood of tears, simply barged into a door! Shyamli took both hands of Kaliyo in her hands, and caressed them. The car started. Her eyes could see nothing. Kaliyo's brimming eyes could also see nothing except trembling water—so he just kept waving in the direction of the sound of the departing car.

In the institute most students were farmers, and several had freshly come from the countryside. And so Kaliyo felt a puff of pride at being a reformed urbanite. His speech, shaped in Shyamli's home, and his well-pressed and well-tailored clothes marked him out like oil in water. And then Kaliyo worked with eight hands, as it were, and so he became the professor's ideal pupil. Dr. Bolman, a famous agro-engineer from Israel who had come for a visit, was greatly impressed by Kaliyo's understanding of farming, and his passion for learning. Kaliyo took a promise from Dr. Bolman that the latter would guide him in creating a fairy-tale farm of his dreams.

Today is the convocation of the Institute of Farming and Dairying. From the morning, Kaliyo is practicing before a mirror how he will bow and thank the Guest of Honour when the diploma is put in his hand, and how he will glue a thick smile on his lips. Sarojben's letter of good wishes, with the message that the family will not be able to attend the function because of Shyamli being indisposed, dampened the surging waves of delight.

Four days later Kaliyo wound up everything and said goodbye to Anand. Kaliyo reached Shyamli's home, and the house turned into the foliage of a mango tree from the unceasing warble of the two friends. Shyamli remembered those days when Kaliyo had first arrived. How silent he was, like a monk! Now Kaliyo spoke incessantly, as if so many tongues had sprung up in Kaliyo's mouth and every tongue was graced by Saraswati, the goddess of learning. In these past months Kaliyo had learnt so much that his ebullience could not be restrained.

"Do you know Shyamli, what I am going to do now?"
"Scrub vessels, clothes, and floor!"
"That you will now do, when you get married and go to your in-laws!"
"I will take you along as an assistant!"
"Come now, stop joking and listen carefully. Hadn't I written to you about my friend Chhagan Patel?"
"Huh . . . yes . . ."
"He has twenty acres of land in Vyara. He is an only son, and needs an intelligent hand."

Shaking Kaliyo's hand with her two hands, Shyamli said, "That is, this hand?"
"These hands are no ordinary hands. Remember that story? That whatever the person's hands touched turned to gold? The same way whatever these hands touch will turn lush green."
"Stay away from me!"
"Shyamli, Israel's Dr. Bolman, too, has promised to guide me."
"But what will Chhagan give you in return?"
"Twenty-five percent share."
"Is this in writing?"
"What's the need for documentation with a friend?"
"Ask Pappa. But if I were in your place I would get it in writing."
Now Kaliyo has his own mind. He does not need to hold anyone's hands for coming to a decision. He goes to Vyara.

He used to keep writing about his numerous experiments. In his last letter he had written:

> *Shyamli!*
>
> *Paddy has grown so abundantly that everyone seeing it gets wide-eyed. Forty tons of paddy is already ripe—another forty tons will be harvested. Tried a new method. The paddy plant matured*

in half the time. There will be two crops this monsoon. Do you know how much money will be my share? Last four months I have just been engrossed in farming. I have done nothing else. Chhagan Patel's farm used to yield no more than twenty tons. Multiply this by four. Shyamli, I will become rich, like you!

Shyamli was lounging in bed, reading Stefan Zweig's stories. A disapproving crow was registering his protest by cawing, until Shyamli's ears, eyes, and mind could take it no more. Shyamli got up four times to get rid off the pesky crow. It returned the fifth time. "A pest of a guest is sure to come", thought Shyamli, and she shut the window.

The evening was about to step on the threshold and run off. The dark waters of the night were rising as the tender light was receding. At that moment a figure, barely able to walk, opened the garden gate and dragged itself to the door.

Somebody came and yet no bell? To put her curiosity to rest, Shyamli rose from the sofa and went to open the door. Kaliyo lay in a heap outside the door. The shocked hands trying to raise the slumped body were assisted by four more and brought the wreck to a sofa. A stethoscope amplified the feeble heartbeats. Medication was administered. Movement appeared after half-an-hour. The throng of eyes experienced relief. The shattered frame turned into a human body. It got a voice. Faces began to converse.

"Who beat you up so badly? Why?"
"Chhagan got me beaten up because he did not want to pay my share."
"You took the beating without a fight?"
"What could I do? I was surrounded by five thugs? Chhagan accused me of theft and they called me a thief and beat me up."

Six hands caressed Kaliyo's head, shoulders, and arms, and gave succour.

When Kaliyo recovered, Shyamli's father asked the question on every one's mind:
"Kaliyo, what will you do now? Shall I find a job for you?"
"No. I will not take a job."

"What do you want to do?"
"Farming."
"Farming is so laborious! And then there is the risk of inadequate or excess rain, excess cold or heat. The whole effort can go waste."
"Father! How much I have learned about farming in these past months! How many new experiments I want to do! I harvested eighty tons of paddy on just twenty acres!"
"How much beating you got because of your obsession with farming!"
"Just because I got a thrashing once, does it mean I will keep on getting beatings throughout life?"
"Do you have land for farming?"
"If the government has some scheme for experimental farming, I could join it. I will enquire with the Sarvodaya people whether they can provide some help. If all else fails I will return to my village and cultivate my small farm."
"Okay, okay . . . Saroj has ten acres of land near Pardi. Her mother died four months back. There is nobody to look after it. You cultivate that land. You have 50% share and I have 50%."
"Let me think. Can we have a legal agreement?"
"Of course!"
"If from my earnings I can accumulate enough, will you be willing to sell the farm to me?"
"Why not?"

Kaliyo laboured hard for four years to bring his scheme to fruition. Today 3000 'graft' mango trees are billowing on his land. How much affection Kaliyo showers on the trees! Every fortnight, there is digging around their trunks so they can 'breathe' better; every three months, manure is applied; every year after harvesting the mangos, there is pruning of branches. In Spring red shoots would appear on the twigs, and seeing those rich reddish mango trees it would be obvious that they are no one else's but Kaliyo's. Whether there is gale or torrential rain, the blossoms keep swaying on the trees. It is Kaliyo's discovery that just as a healthy person can withstand infection, a healthy tree always retains its flowers and fruit despite inclement weather. After eating the mangos of Kaliyo's farm, other mangos taste flat.

Even in the mango tree's shade, with Bolman's scientific technique Kaliyo has planted numerous commercial plants. Kaliyo has erected a windmill on a windy, high portion of the farm. This keeps on supplying electricity without interruption. Kaliyo's little house is in the farm's centre. It is made of earth and lime, but it is hard like stone.

Despite Kaliyo being a 'foreigner' from Dungarpur, the villagers like him on account of his friendliness and ready willingness to help others. When Kaliyo requested the hand of Sona, the village headman Maganbhai's daughter, Maganbhai agreed to a wedding the very next month. Being pragmatic, he felt that one should not go to wash one's face when Laxmi, the goddess of fortune comes round to put a chandla[30] on one's forehead.

Kaliyo posts the first invitation to Shyamli; the second to Shyamli's parents; and then to his home, to his parents and brothers.

The invitees arrive. On their faces is the verdure of pleasure. Kaliyo changes from being single into a couple.

You may have seen many fields. But if you go to Pardi, don't miss seeing Kaliyo's farm. Kaliyo has given every speck of dust a green voice!

30 An auspicious circular mark, usually red

TUFAN

Beyond the village's outskirts is a decrepit Shiva temple. A flag, red as chanothi,[31] flutters at its crest. Some distance away is a river. Not much water. On the banks, small and big pits, and caverns covered by vegetation. They look as if they have hidden their faces in purdah. However far one stretches one's sight, no habitations are visible that can give comfort to the lonely temple.

A bearded middle-aged man wearing just a dhoti,[32] with prematurely silver hair, is sitting on the steps of the temple. He keeps putting his hand to his temple, his eyebrows creased in anxiety and anger, and keeps muttering, "Where has he gone?" He is the temple priest. The sun has already set. Piercing the darkness with a lantern, the priest descends the temple's steps. Just that moment, from the distance wafts the voice of a twelve year old boy. He is coming towards the priest on the trot. He pants as he calls. Getting near, the boy hugs the priest. "Father! Don't get angry—but today I saw on the other side of the river such fine blue stones! It took a long time to dig them out of the ground." He takes out small rocks and shows them in the lantern's light. In a huff, ignoring the rocks the priest climbs the temple's steps. The son follows.

All four feet enter the temple. And then begins the daily ritual of the father scolding and the son pacifying him. Voices subside.

The sun has yet to open its eye; but Tufan is already up. There is a tiny enclosure in the rear portion of the temple. Tufan has stuffed in it his

---

31 The red seed of a berry

32 Lower garment commonly worn by Indian males

collection of soils, stones, feathers, dried flowers, barks, leaves, stones of fruits, seed, pieces of honeycomb. In a corner is a large iron mortar.

Earlier, Tufan and his father lived in the forest. At ten Tufan could identify instantly plants with medicinal value from amongst similar looking plants; the father had taught him their properties. Tufan was used to spending hours in the sun without food or drink. Once enough stock of medicinal herbs accumulated, father and son traveled to a nearby village, sold it off and bought from the proceeds their daily necessities. The population of this village was around 5000, and a mart was held in it every Wednesday. All sorts of handcrafted wares were on display. The father would get a seat at the mart to sell his nostrums, his silver beard a-flutter like a flag. Tufan's mind, hungry for human contact, would revolve around those whose looks and style appealed to his eyes. Cloistered inside the hut from birth, and living with just one person, Tufan would get exhilarated aligning his pulse with the throb of the multitude. His heart would droop a little at the thought that with eventide he would again get stuck in his little hut.

All of a sudden his father developed a cyst in his thigh. The feet refused to perform their duties. The noble lines of the face drawn by the Artist became contorted in the face of pain. "Who would look after Tufan when I am gone?" The thought caused a short circuit in the father's mind. His heart experienced a wrench at the thought of leaving the forest after years of myriad associations. But this umbrella that had got overturned was no longer capable of bearing the onslaught of a downpour.

Tufan's fiery will decided the course of action: "We can no longer live in this jungle. We must go to a place where you can be treated, and I can go to school."

The father was in agony at forsaking the hut in the jungle, his sanctuary for the past twenty years. How could one uproot and wind up so many years of life that had spread like creepers around forest trees? But a portion of his consciousness could break away from the tangle of vines, and he set forth, taking the support of the staff that was his son. After roaming for days, all four feet climbed a temple's steps one evening. They rested there for the night. And stayed on.

Few came to the temple for worship, as the temple was about a mile away from the nearby village. The father and the son repaired the temple. The temple, painted white with lime and with a red flag fluttering from its summit, began to attract the village folk. Gradually they began to visit regularly. They would leave behind a little money as well as provisions, and this would suffice for the two. The cyst disappeared with the salve provided by the village's Hakimchacha.[33] The dejected feet again began to smile.

Today the sound of pounding has been heard since the morning. Rock has had to be pounded into a fine powder. Tufan keeps pounding, perspiring heavily. Two decisive eyes stand out in a body that is bony due to malnutrition. Thus do minutes-hours-days-years keep getting ground inside the mortar into pigments.

Those coming to the temple for worship were attracted to Tufan. He chatted with them with relish and verve. He would humorously recount the memorable experiences of his stay of ten years in the forest, and the listeners would get into fits of laughter. The village kids of Tufan's age began to yearn for his company. They regularly began to congregate in the temple's courtyard after school was over. On their insistence Tufan entered school. The kind-hearted in the village readily bought books and gifted them to Tufan. But in just a month he began to express his lack of confidence in the education he was getting.

One evening he told the gathering on the temple plinth: "The teaching here is like the shell of groundnuts—is this edible? Once in a while you get a nut in the shell—but who wants to waste time from morning to evening for just a few nuts?" The reason for Tufan finding the teaching so worthless was that Tufan was put in the third grade, though mentally he was on par with his age group.

33 A hakim is a practitioner of the Muslim form of indigenous medicine

Chinu had become Tufan's friend during the past six months. Chinu's father had a store in the village that sold all sorts of wares. Chinu strongly persuaded Tufan to continue in school, but after six months Tufan dropped out. The father protested, but Tufan told him in plain words: "It takes me an hour to learn what they take eight hours to teach at school, and I am not going to be imprisoned in four walls for eight hours."
"Son! You could get a job in the village if you were to study some more."
"I and a job! I will not work under any one."
"And who will work under some one raw like you?"
"I will start my own business of selling colours."
"Are colours so short in the world that people will buy yours?"
"You'll see that my colours are sold and those of others remain piled up."

Self-confidence rang in Tufan's voice. The father was familiar both with Tufan's Chanakya[34] will and Chanakya mind. So he dropped the matter of Tufan's continuing in school.

Chinu used to come every evening. With gusto Tufan learnt to read and write from him. Once when Chinu was explaining the rules of spelling, Tufan was utterly delighted at grasping their logic. He threw away the book, got up, and leaping about, delightedly recited a rhyme: 'Chinu Chotli/ sows grammar's seed/ the seed are so fresh/ I am happy indeed.'

Whenever Tufan intuited something unfamiliar, he experienced a flash in his mind, and romped about from the headiness of the illumination. Chinu could not understand this madness. What was there to dance about from learning when to use a short or a long vowel? But it was because of this liveliness of mind that all the 'birds' used to gather at the temple's porch.

The night huddled in a freezing cold. Tufan got up and went to his small chamber to see how the colour he had made in a clay pot the previous evening had come out. For quite some time he had been attempting to

34 The fourth century BC mentor of Emperor Chandragupta Maurya, who had vowed to destroy the Nanda dynasty and succeeded through his indomitable will and Machiavellian mind

make a blue colour, but the colour would not yield the blueness he had visualized. Tufan turned into the hue of heavens when he saw in the candle light the blue he had wanted—that of a choppy sea! Stepping out into the darkness, he set off for the river.

For the last several days Tufan has been boiling gum, wax, clay, leaves and what not in metal pots. He is thrilled at seeing the rainbow colours created through his ingenuity and effort. Chemical colours are dime a dozen in the market, but who else can make such vibrant *natural* colours! With great pride he pours colours into bottles. Some are for use on paper and some on cloth. Humming to himself eulogies of the colours, he sticks labels on the bottles. The bottles are carefully placed in the drawers of a wooden box he has made with his own hands.

The father did not take much interest in all this colour-making activity. He used to get incensed at his son wasting his time over something as useless as colours. One day, as soon as the father got up in the morning, Tufan went to him with his box, showed it to him and said, "I am going to Sinhnagar in the 10 o'clock bus. I am sure I will be able to sell my colours there." The father expressed his doubts with a slight curl of his lips; but the mouth blessed, "Go and return with success"!

Sinhnagar was about a hundred miles from Tufan's village. A well-known painter resided there. Tufan had read about him in a newspaper. For a long time Tufan had wanted to meet him; but he could not gather up the courage to barge into a stranger's place. Tufan knew nothing about painting and his ignorance about the art in which his colours could be used bothered him. "The painter will dip his brush in the colours and rapidly paint some lines; and suddenly the mute colours will turn eloquent. And then he will ask, 'Where did you get these amazing colours from'?" How many times a day he re-lived this fantasy!

It was just an hour before departure. His mind was hopping around in the excitement of going. At the same time, the thought that he had never left his village and the prospect of going, all alone, to a confusing city to meet a stranger produced a sinking feeling in his stomach.

At the moment for going, Tufan bowed low before his father for blessings. For the first time the father felt that his son had ceased to be a child, and did not need the crutch of his fingers. Rather, he needed the support of his son. It was as if his responsibility as a parent had ended.

"Father, do not worry. I may have to stay on for a day or two."
"Do you have enough money?"
"Yes"
"Take care."

In all these years the father and the son had never been separated this way. Every day of Tufan's life had risen in the presence of his father. How will the next day be without this loving spectator of his life? At bed time Tufan used to sit on his father's cot and press his feet to alleviate their fatigue. Who will hush to sleep those aching feet tonight? The prospect of separation stung the hearts of both.

The village's bus-stop was merely the shade of a big banyan tree. Tufan put his box on the ground and sat on it carefully to avoid putting all his weight on it. Ten minutes passed. No bus. "The bus driver must have found an acquaintance on the way. He must have been busy having tea or liquor, or in answering nature's call." He sat musing thus. After a while the bus did come.

Tufan sat in a bus for the first time. He got 'high' watching the fleeing world from his elevation. His eyes went forwards and backwards, not missing any sight within or without the bus. But they tired after a couple of hours. So did his body, from tossing about in the jerky bus ride. Then he fell asleep. The bus emptied at Sinhnagar, and the conductor shook Tufan's shoulder. Tufan got up with a start.

When he emerged from the lap of the bus he became aware that now he was entirely on his own in a completely alien place. He felt afraid, and he perspired. But he suppressed his fears, and asked with confidence a young man by his side:
"Brother! Where does Vasudev Painter live?"
"How would I know where he stays in this big town? What is his address?"

Tufan took out a slip of paper from his pocket and put it into the other's hand.
"He lives quite far from here. Take a rickshaw."
Tufan had never hailed a rickshaw, so he hesitated. But then he clapped to stop one of these irate hags.
"I want to go to Bangadi Vada at Zampa Bazar."
The rickshaw driver signaled to Tufan to get inside. The rickshaw speeded off, barely avoiding ramming into pedestrians.
"Here is Bangadi Vada, sir!"
Tufan got down in confusion. His confusion was about how to make the payment.
"Brother! How much is the fare?"
"Two rupees."
"So much?!"
"I don't run the meter with my hand. Just pay according to the meter. Don't waste my time."

That moment humiliated Tufan; the next raised his determination.

Smiling, Tufan said, "I sat in the rickshaw for the first time so I didn't know how to read the meter. Could you please teach me?" The rickshaw driver looked archly at his slovenly tailored pant and shirt, and smirked. Tufan was unaware of this city way of assessing people, so he did not grasp the rickshaw driver's body language. As if obliging, the rickshaw driver rudely explained the fare calculation. Tufan immediately understood, and happily paid two rupees.

He asked a group of three persons standing on the road, "Where does Vasudev Painter live?"
"There—inside that big gate," the three mouths spoke nearly simultaneously. There was a sentry at the gate. "I want to meet Vasudev Painter," he said. At this, he was led to a studio.

The painter, his eyes glued to a large canvas, and a painting in mind, was moving the brush here and there on the white sky. Not wanting to intrude, Tufan sat at a distance in a corner. He got engrossed observing the way the painter held the brush in his fingers, dipped it in colour and then jerked the brush to remove the excess fluid, how he retreated some distance from the canvas to see whether he had got the effect he had desired, and the various angles his neck assumed while doing all this.

After finishing, the painter turned to go out. His gaze fell upon Tufan huddling in a corner. "Who?" The query was etched in his eyes. Tufan felt like a mouse wanting to escape into a burrow. But that wish was only momentary. Tufan forced himself to get up and greet the painter with a namaskar.[35] "I live outside Ambli-Pimpli village and I have come to show these colours I have made," he said, a bit hesitantly.

The painter was struck by Tufan's directness. He approached Tufan.
"You make the colours yourself?"
"I have been making them for many years. Please see . . ."

Tufan opened the wooden box, and the painter sat down to look at the colours more carefully. One by one he opened a bottle to see the colour. His face beamed. He got up to retrieve his bundle of brushes and paper, returned, and again sat next to the box of colours. He dipped a brush in each bottle and made it dance on the paper. All the colours marked their presence.

"This red is amazing—how did you make it? Such a red used to be made centuries back in China. I have not seen it anywhere recently."
"A red stone is occasionally found in the crevices on the banks of the river of my village. This red comes out after I powder it and pour liquefied gum of babul[36], silvery mica, chichuka seeds, and many other things into it. Then I boil all these together, cool, strain the substance, and bury it underground for a month. It takes about a month-and-a-half to make this colour."
"Are you the son of a colour-maker?"
"My father hates my making colours. He is a temple priest."
"From whom did you learn to make colours?"
"I learnt on my own."
"Who gave my name to you?"
"I had read an article on you in a newspaper. I want to sell these colours—do you need them?"

35 Literally, greeting by bowing
36 A thorny tree

"I want all these colours; but not one bottle. I want ten bottles of each colour."
He looked at the painter in disbelief.
"Leave these colours here. I will later come to your village for other colours. How much is to be paid?"
"Four rupees per bottle, but if you think this is too high then you can reduce a little."
"High? These are even cheaper than chemical colours. How many bottles can you produce in a month?"
"I can't estimate. But can my colours sell?"
"Why not? I just bought them."
"But where else can I sell them?"
"Can't think right away, but textile printing is highly developed in Sinhnagar. The businessmen here may buy your colours for dying cloth."

Vasudevbhai's eyes narrowed in some thought. Suddenly, ashamed of his absent-mindedness he said, "We talked so much, but I did not ask your name!"
"Tufan."
The painter saw lightning prancing in the eyes of the speaker. The artist's soul was dazzled by its flashes.

To Tufan the world felt inviting like a meadow. He was ecstatic at the thought of reposing on it. Till then Tufan had encountered innumerable thorny bushes and trees, and the thorns had frequently drawn Tufan's blood. However, he had never come across thorny people.

Tufan had the feel of a city for the first time, and he wanted to explore it through its thoroughfares. The painter took Tufan for a ride in his car. Tufan felt like someone sitting in a rocket for the first time. The artist showed with his artist's sight all the fine spots of the city—the palace of a Rajput[37] king, the mausoleum of a sultan, the temple of the Swaminarayan sect, a college. The eyes of the artist enhanced their magnificence.

When they sat down for dinner, Tufan felt awkward sitting in a chair. Though his stomach juices seethed from the food's aroma, he could not

37 Member of the warrior caste

enjoy the food without being, as his wont, able to eat with his hands and sitting cross-legged on the floor. He did relish, however, observing the painter's table manners, how the painter sat, held the spoon, munched with his lips closed—but the fun of eating was ruined by his having to imitate the painter's table manners. The painter's manners were so graceful, while he thought his own were so crude!

Tufan's chair was some distance from the table, and while taking morsels from the thali[38], something or the other fell down. The painter's displeasure was plain. Tufan gathered up his slipping courage and said, "Vasudevbhai! This is the first time I am dining while sitting on a chair—I am finding this very difficult. Couldn't you please coach me?"

The training of table manners began. Tufan learnt fast—after all, his name meant storm. Never before did the painter have such a pupil!

When Tufan set off early next morning, the painter said with feeling, "I'll come to get the colours in a mouth, so make as many as you can. Take these sixty rupees for the colours." Tufan was thrilled at the touch of the wealth that was his by right. On the way home how many times he pressed the money in his pocket to ensure that it was still there! In the excitement the journey passed quickly, and the passage from the village to the temple turned out to be short. Breathlessly he climbed the steps of the temple. He put the money in his father's hands and threw his arms around him. The flag of victory fluttered in the father's eyes; the victor, after all, was his very own!

Words tumbled forth, as Tufan rapidly recounted his experiences. After hearing out Tufan, the worldly-wise father said, "Son! You have hardly met people to be able to judge their character! Don't think that those who appear good are necessarily so."

"Father! When you meet him you only will say that you haven't seen such a person before." Saying "Okay, okay", the father patted the son's back.

38 Metal plate for eating a meal

The eighteen years old Tufan has no time for fun and frolic. The whole day goes in collecting gum, seed, flowers, bark and so forth. Then time runs off while pounding stones and earth, and boiling these into a viscous liquid. Tufan is engaged in a whirl of activities all day. His friend Chinu Chotli also joins him. Chinu observes the process intently. At the end of the month six hundred bottles of colour are ready.

On seeing the painter ascend the temple's steps, Tufan rushed down, grabbed his hand affectionately, and took him to his small enclosure.

"Just see how many colours I have prepared!"
"I thought you would have forgotten to make colours and you were whiling away your time loitering in the crevices on the river's banks!"
"Once I said I would make them, I would—and I would never forget."
Tufan introduced his father.
"Tufan had described you in such minute detail that I would have recognized you even on the road."
Tufan said, a little diffidently, "There is nothing in my village like what you have in your city to show you . . . but can I take you to see the crevices?"
"Sure."

Seeing Tufan leap excitedly from rock to rock, the painter experienced a surge of many-hued sensations,. The brush of the painter might have captured all this hopping, but his feet despaired!

At night the painter succumbed to the insistence of the father and the son that he dine with them; but his bending down to eat was reminiscent of the Panchatantra[39*] story of the stork trying to eat kheer[40**] from a plate!

39 A compendium of fables with moral lessons.
40 A milk-based sweet

"Can you supply these many bottles every month?"
"Why not?"
"Have you seen that small shop outside my place? The colours can be kept there for sale. My students and friends will buy only from there. My painter friends liked your colours a lot—but the colours must always be of this quality."
"They will improve as I become more adept."
"Here! Take these two thousand four hundred rupees for the six hundred bottles."

The painter extended his hand to give the money to the father. The father had never seen so much money in his life. His hand got petrified. The painter put the money into his hand with feeling.
"Now open a bank account in Tufan's name."
"Okay!"
"Tufan, some day, do bring your father over to see the city."
The father and the son levitated in delight.

The next month Tufan went to Sinhnagar and delivered the colours on date, as also the month after. Tufan's colours got acceptance in Sinhnagar due to his timely delivery, their quality, and the delight on the buyer's face that acted as an advertisement.

In the fourth month Tufan was encircled on all sides. He was at a loss as to which difficulty to address, and how. He used to make orange from the stem of the Parijat flowers during the monsoon. Tufan had dried the flowers and stored them in sacks, and these were just about exhausted. The availability of red rock in the crevices had greatly dwindled. Even the gum from various trees was now in short supply. Chinu Chotli had stolen Tufan's technique. He had started making the colours himself and selling them in his shop. How to tackle all these problems single-handedly?

Chinu had not allowed even a hint of his action to reach Tufan. Since Chinu had not turned up for eight days Tufan went over to Chinu's shop. Colours like his had been displayed in the shop to catch everyone's attention. For the first time Tufan experienced man's thorniness. His body shook as he wondered about whose thorns would be piercing him next.

He spent sleepless nights. The sparkle in his eyes dimmed. His appetite died. His face paled. Tufan's father could not comprehend his anxiety.

"If you cannot supply the colours this month, don't! Why must you take this so much to heart?"

"Vasudevbhai has been able to get the shopkeeper to store my colours after so much trouble! Should customers go back without them? The shopkeeper will store others' colours. My standing will be lost. Who will then trust me?"

For days Tufan was ground down by anxiety.

Tufan had saved about ten thousand rupees. With a surge of resilience, Tufan began to consider how to put that money to work. If you can ground grain in a mortar, can't you ground stones in it, too? Can't one design a furnace in which material can be liquefied without manual stirring? Slowly a new plan took shape in his mind. But he needed to test it before implementing it.

A deeply ashamed Tufan went to Vasudevbhai to explain that he would not be able to supply the goods for two months. "The colours will not be available?" The pitch of Vasudevbhai's voice leaped. "If you cannot supply the materials for two months, who will wait for you in the third month?"
"So far I have paid attention only to making the colours; but for providing regular supplies it is necessary to keep in mind many other factors. It will take me some time to make all this systematic. I want your advice."

Vasudevbhai saw the grief on Tufan's face. Tears began to well up in Toofan's eyes. Vasudevbhai's heart melted. Both sat together, shared their ideas, and evolved a new initiative.

Vasudevbhai gave the name of an engineer. Rusibhai rapidly sketched out the sort of machinery relevant for Tufan's colour business. Tufan applied his mind to it and suggested some modifications. Tufan briefed Rusibhai about the difficulty of procuring raw materials. Rusibhai suggested the name of Khimji Jadavji. This firm was selling a lot of its goods to Ayurveda[41] pharmacies. Tufan left for Mumbai to meet the owners. To get there, he first got into a bus for Visnagar. This was the first time he had seen such a large railway station. An occasional train stopped near his village, that, too, for just a minute, and on the station there was just a board for Chincholiya, the name of the village, and one bench. Tufan got frightened seeing five bridges arching over Visnagar station. Where was he to board the train for Mumbai? So many trains were parked.

Shaking off his fear, he asked a T.T.,[42] "Sir, I have to catch the train for Mumbai. How do I get in?"

"Purchase a ticket for Mumbai from that ticket window there, go to Platform Number 3, and get into Saurashtra Express."

Reciting repeatedly the platform number and the name of the train to learn them by heart, Tufan got to Saurashtra Express. But now which bogey to get into? The door of every bogey was crammed like a honeycomb with human bees. For some minutes he ran from one door to another. Once or twice he entreated, "Let me enter." But the human bees placidly blocked his entry.

Then Tufan summoned all his strength and courage and shouted: "Move aside . . .". Gripping in one hand his metal bag and swiping his other hand from side to side, he lowered his head and bored into the crowd. He could get in, but there was no place to sit.
He thought of a trick to get a seat. Father, mother, and son were comfortably seated on one bench. Tufan got close to them. He smiled at the son. Then he asked, "What is your name? What are you studying?" Then, as if he had just chanced to see the boy's palm, he said, "Let me see your palm. Your future can make even a minister jealous! You will study a lot, indeed!"

These sentences worked wonders! The parents immediately made space for Tufan to sit. After that, eight other palms presented themselves to Tufan. When Mumbai came, a passenger who was happy with Tufan's

41 India's indigenous medical system
42 A railway official

joyful predictions, dropped him in his taxi to Jadavji Khimji's shop, saying, "Oh! It is on my way."

Khimji was by now already a guest of God. But Tufan talked business with Jadavji. "I can meet all your requirements for Parijat flowers and the gum of babul and neem trees and so forth, except for stones. But you will have to sign a year's contract. I will dispatch the goods by truck between the first and the third of every month, and you will have to take delivery by paying cash."
"I will let you know in a week."
"Let me know in time; otherwise you may not get next month's materials."
"Alright, Jadavjibhai. This trade was of your father's, too?"
"Oh no! My father was a farmer. But he was very fond of growing plants for medicinal uses. We have never swallowed any pills while growing up. Whenever we fell sick, father would procure a few green leaves from the farm and give them to us to chew. We just learnt by observing father."
"But how did you get into this trade?"
"From the beginning I had the temperament of a trader, and so I put mine and my father's brains together and got into this trade. And how did you get into this colour business?"
"My father and I used to live in the jungle. He was an expert on medicinal plants and materials and I learned a lot by being with him. But like you I too had the temperament of a trader, so got into this colour business. Jadavjibhai! Did you get set in your business immediately, or did you have some bad times, too?"
"Friend! Thieves have four eyes. They can adulterate so expertly that even a knowledgeable person like me can get fooled! Once Harihar Pharmacy returned goods worth four hundred thousand rupees, claiming they were fake. After that I stopped buying from the swindler. But he nearly drove me bankrupt, he did!"
"Then what did you do?"
"Such things keep happening in business. Once again I got going with hard work. It is quite a special pleasure to rise again after a fall."
"Who can teach me how to judge plants?"
"The Ayurveda pharmacists have a complete knowledge about this. But I don't know whether they will teach you!"
"Do you know any stone merchant?"

"Meet Rameshchandra Raichand near Chandni Chabutara. He is a friend. Do give my reference."

Whoever he met would point to someone else. This way Tufan met as many as fifty persons. Tufan felt exhilarated by this interactive game. He thought, "Now I can tell Father I have met so many that my eyes can judge them instantly.

"That Rameshchandra—how he shifted his eyes when he told me the price of the rocks! He coughed a little and said: 'This price is very reasonable. You are Jadavjibhai's friend. How can I charge a higher price to you?' Absolute liar!

"That pharmacist says to me, 'If the neem tree's gum turns green when you boil it in water then know that it is genuine.' I have gathered this gum for years and boiled it. It has never turned green! Why would they lie like this? Why don't they just say straight, 'We don't want to teach you!'"

Where to get the money was the biggest question. What could he do with his mere ten thousand? A thakor[43] lived in the village. He was said to be very well-to-do, but also tight fisted. Tufan thought, "What's the harm in trying?" One day, taking a bag of fragrant tobacco crushed into powder by his father, Tufan went to meet the thakor.

The thakor was sitting on a mattress, reclining on pillows and smoking a hukkah. He wore a turban and his gaze was slightly lowered, as if he was 'high'. But when he looked up, his eyes revealed him to be a shrewd man of the world. A man standing behind the thakor held a cloth to swat pestering flies.

Tufan bowed, greeted, put the bag at the feet of the thakor, and said, "How are you, sir?"
"Son! I am as well as my age will allow. How are you?"
"What can be any complaint at my age? I am in the colour business."

43 Member of a warrior caste

"How is it going?"
"Okay. But if I can get some money fuel, it can take off."
"Ah! So you have come to borrow!"
"I had not seen you for a long time, so I wanted to meet you, and also to invite you to join my business."
"At this age how can a bullock be yoked?"
"You don't have to do anything. You have just to invest money and receive the agreed upon share of profit."
"Why should I put at risk the security of the money lying in my safe?"
"Sir, for you it will be only a drop out of the ocean; but all I have amounts to just ten thousand rupees."

Tufan put his bank passbook in the thakor's hands.

"Oh, oh! The temple priest has accumulated ten thousand!"
"Sir, not as a temple priest. I have earned the money in the colour trade. Just four months business earned me ten thousand. It is a golden goose. There is plenty of demand. But I need capital to make the products."

The thakor tried to penetrate Tufan's eyes to ascertain his integrity. They found no obstacle of deceit.

"Please see this certificate of Vasudevbhai, the Sinhnagar painter." Vasudevhai had given a typed certificate that Tufan's colours were of top quality and Vasudevbhai insisted on using only Tufan's colours.
"If you keep the money in the safe it will remain the same. But if you give it to me it will quickly double."

Generally, the thakor never even offered water to any visitor. But he insisted on Tufan having tea. The village was stunned to learn that the thakor, who sat tight over his safe in padmasana[44*], had signed an agreement to provide rupees twenty-five thousand to Tufan.

Thirty-five thousands were in the kitty. But the money was not enough. Tufan started making an effort to procure a bank loan. Dhanjibhai, the manager of the local branch of State Bank of India turned out to be a friend of Vasudevbhai. On Vasudevbhai's personal guarantee he gave a

44 A yogic sitting posture

loan of rupees fifty thousand to Tufan to put up a plant for producing colours.

Thus was the money puran[45] concluded.

The father found out an auspicious hour for the factory's inauguration. In just a month bottles of many different colours started coming out and being sold. The production train went fast for six months. By then the population of bottles multiplied so fast that the problem of excess stocks arose.

Sales were very good in Sinhnagar. But how much could just Sinhnagar absorb? Tufan's colours were probably getting sold also in nearby towns, but there was no information about this. If sales were not enough, how to pay the workers, procure raw materials, and pay the interest on the bank loan?

Tufan was foxed. For a few days he could not figure out what to do. As if this was not enough, the thakor sent his muscle men to recover his dues. While Tufan was sitting at night on a temple step, one of them struck him hard on the back with a stick.

A prolonged scream rushed out from Tufan's throat. In agony, Tufan dragged himself to where his father was. The father was panic-stricken.

Barely had Tufan recovered from the beating, the craftsmen and labourers set up a clamour for not getting paid in time. Tufan patiently explained the situation. What is more, he asked for their advice as if they were his partners.

"I too am a labourer and a craftsman who works with both hands—just like you. I am not a wealthy owner. We are all partners in this small factory. We will all be penniless if it closes down. Your pay will be a little irregular for the next two months. But I am confident that with your

45 Ancient religious epic

cooperation we will pull through. If the plant runs well I will give double the normal one month bonus on this Dipavali[46]."

Tufan could ease the load on the minds of his craftsmen and workers through his transparency and genuine concern.

After sorting out most matters, Tufan went to Sinhnagar to seek Vasudevbhai's advice. Then Tufan, grabbing his colours in both arms, zipped through numerous towns. He met legions of merchants. He met principals of art schools. He met painters. He impressed them with his paeans of praise for his colours. He put his darling bottles in the hands of all those prospective grooms who had extended their arms! The bottles, languishing for months in Tufan's warehouse, found worthy duty in their new homes.

Today is Deepavali. After feeding a sumptuous meal to his staff members, who, like ascetics, have endured deprivations for months, Tufan concludes his Rajsuya Yagna[47] of victory. After the meal, Tufan puts two months of bonus pay in envelopes and hands them over to his staff. In the end he speaks only two sentences:

"I will never forget what you have done for me. I wish most heartily that you too create something of your own, and I will help you all I can."

Now Tufan has no time to go to nooks and crannies to gather rocks. But in his dreams, little Tufan still forages for rocks, climbs trees to gather gum in his pockets, collects vibrantly tinted flowers, and dries them in the sun.

46 The festival of light
47 A sacrificial rite performed in ancient times by emperors to celebrate conquest, followed by sumptuous gifts to the subjects.

MILLENNIUM OLD AHALYA

The peaks, craning their white necks for better hearing, had assembled for a chat. Normally they would be engrossed in cosmic gossip, such as the affair of a male star with a female star. But that day the topic of discussion was the Earth, and the talk had taken a controversial turn: which of the Earth's epochs was the best? A controversy raged among the summits. Some said, "The best was the 'Sat Yuga'[48]. The sages could then converse at will with us through their yogic power. Contemporary humans do fly around in the sky; but they care little about us." Some said, "No epoch like the present Kali Yuga[49]. Man has eclipsed even the gods. He can live where he wills—in the sky, in the nether world, in water, on the land. So what if he does not converse with us. But for the Earth this is the best epoch." Some said: "You forget that the Earth means not just man. Have you ever seen such a misfortune for the Earth? Humans have made the Earth bare!"

Slicing through this talk came a huge silvery flying saucer. It descended in whirlwind fashion, planted three feet in the ice field, and stood there. All the peaks trained their gazes on it.

Shortly, five persons exited from it. It seemed impossible to tell them apart, for they seemed to be cast from the same mould. Nor was it clear whether their bodies had clothes on them or not. Something like an aura surrounded their bodies—as if they had a mysterious armour on them. Like a sleeper inside a mosquito net, who looks like a blur in dim light, the bodies of the five were hazy.

---

48 The epoch of truth, morality, and prosperity.

49 The present 'evil' epoch.

These five figures sometimes got close to one another, sometimes distanced themselves from one another, and sometimes paired off. They showed no feelings of closeness for one another, for they were not seen to hold each other's hands, or to rest their hands on each other's shoulders, or thump one another's backs in happy camaraderie. The trampled snow was eloquent, but not one word issued from their lips.

One person was peering with great curiosity at something near a foot of the fat, broad saucer squatting on the ice. A robot descended near the huge foot of the saucer, close to where the person was peering. As if following a telepathic command, the robot started digging around the foot of the saucer. The robot exposed a scarf made of red bandhani and handed it to the person. The person turned the scarf around several times and observed it carefully. Blunt fingers felt the fabric clumsily, as if they had forgotten the softness of touch. Without any call at all, the rest converged near the foot of the saucer, and formed a small circle. An effort seemed to be on to explain/understand something. The whole scene was like a silent movie.

The robot again started digging at the spot. This time a leather boot emerged. None of the five had worn anything on their feet, but they knew that their great—great—great—great grandparents used to wear something like this for protecting their feet. Their anthropological museums contained collections of many different types of sandal and shoe. The robot kept digging with a sharp implement. It dug out a tattered snow-suit. Next it pulled out a haversack from the ice. It contained apparel, and also a comb, a purse, a glass, a small steel platter, a pen, and a diary. None of these were of use to the five. They had value only as relics. Each of the five scanned the jottings in the diary, but not comprehending them, they put the diary back into the haversack.

Now three robots started digging. A human toe peeped out. The digging stopped as if in response to an order, and the robots ferried from the spaceship a strangely shaped machine. They placed it near the toe and turned it on. A whole frozen body came out from the layers of ice. It was a girl of about twenty. Her long black hair were braided into a bun. Though she was lifeless, the curves of her body were still eloquent.

Eyes would have popped in astonishment if any five of a bygone era had seen something like this. There would have been a commotion! But these five seemed to be committed to silence. Still, from the slight rises and falls of their limbs they seemed a little excited. As if the body was priceless, it was placed with great care in their vehicle.

Like an arrow, the saucer streaked away to its home base. It steadied its feet and stood on the ground. This was not some other planet. It was the Earth only, but the region was difficult to tell. The land seemed totally barren. The sky was empty of birds, bereft of calls and the rush of wings. No plants flowered on the ground, nor did toddlers scamper about. Nor was there the passage of seasons. There were structures though, as far as the eyes could scan. Some were high like a ladder for the sky; some, long like the Nile; some, vast and cylindrical like the cosmic egg of Brahma; some, demonically triangular. In short, there was a forest of exotic structures, created, though, by combining basic shapes.

But there are no windows to these structures to allow us to see what is going on in them, nor to allow those within to see what is happening in the world outside. But then, what is the use of having windows? The people living inside these structures feel no urge to peep outside. Only accidentally do the Sun's rays intrude here—these people have created their own suns for illumination. Like Alladin's djinn, their suns are presented at the press of a button. Their lumens are also under their control. Turn a knob, and a sun can be brightened—or dimmed. In their computers they have programmed various routes and flows of air. The wind can be made to dance in a circle as per one programme; or flow, dip and sway like a scarf as per another. You can enjoy diverse currents just by pressing different buttons.

Here the body is totally at ease. There are no mosquitoes, no bugs, no heat, and no cold. Press a button to get the weather you want and at will you can raise the temperature, lower it, and raise or lower humidity. The body does not have to suffer any pain. As soon as any organ deteriorates, one goes to the body repair workshop. You lie down, and presto, you are repaired! There is nothing like pain here—but then there is also no exhilaration that humans knew earlier.

To ancients sweating in the oven of the summer, the green, soothing breeze blowing through a canopy would splash pleasure on all their pores—but no one here has experienced this. To enjoy that cool breeze in the summer one has to experience suffocation from heat! Here there are just no shortages. Therefore there is no feeling of affliction through deprivation, and hence there is no leap of joy from getting something after experiencing want. Here everybody's mind is calm, like the still waters of a lake. No mind dances in exuberance on the cresting waves of the ocean.

Everybody here carries a small gadget, which greatly speeds up physical movements. They don't raise their feet to walk. That would be such a waste of energy and time! Amazingly, they *slide* over surfaces.

On the streets there are various sorts of vehicle. But there are none the ancients could have recognized. There is congestion in the sky. How many vehicles whoosh around there! How many strange signals are there for traffic control! The moon and the stars seem pale before the glitter of their vehicles and traffic signals. Of course nobody here writes poetry, and no one appreciates it. So they need no moon or stars for metaphors!

On this part of the Earth there is a nearly festive commotion today. In ancient times, people would sprinkle colour on one other during a festival, dance, beat the drum during a song, shout slogans, and dress up and go out with frolicking eyes—nothing like that here. But today a lot of people have come out of the structures. This is no small event! People are sitting, standing, or peeping out of galleries in bunches. The reason for this festivity is that they have acquired an amazing relic—an ancient girl!

There are screens everywhere, but not like the ones in ancient theatres. They are transparent; they cannot even be seen! The scenes look so vivid—as if they are appearing before one's very eyes. On the screens the girl is seen lying down on a bed in a laboratory. Around her are the five persons who brought her. They are busy doing an experiment. These five are distinguished scientists of the place. Without speaking, they are explaining to their viewers what they are up to, and what they will shortly be doing.

The scientists bring alive the frozen girl as easily as earlier one could turn on a light by repairing a blown fuse. The closed eyelashes of the girl and the eyes beneath them begin to move. After a while, the eyes open. For a while they keep opening and closing. Then she rubs her eyes and gets up. She feels frightened, seeing people around her who look only partially like humans. She screams. The scientists seem shocked by that sound. For a moment the girl feels that like Gulliver she has blundered into another world.

She scratched her head to remember. Last, she was trapped in a snowstorm while climbing the Himalayas with her friends. Did these people kidnap her from there? Or, she had slid down a crevasse and her soul had entered one of the supernatural realms described in the scriptures? She passed all ten of her fingers over her face as if she was trying to recognize it. She felt that the face was as she had known it. She bent down to look at her feet. She folded her fingers into the form of a parrot, a butterfly, and a fish. Now she knew for sure that she was the same old person.

Slowly she got up. Trembling, she asked the non-human looking person next to her, "Who are you? Where am I?" Her voice filled the deathly silent room. The others remained stuck in silence. Again she asked. Again, only silence. Seized by fear and anger, the girl screamed: "Do you hear me or are you deaf? Or you have no tongue at all?" The girl's shouted questions struck the mute persons. They returned like the waves of the ocean repulsed by the boulders on the coast. She felt like shaking the person standing next to her. But she was afraid that she might be scorched or electrocuted by the aura enveloping the person's body.

She began to cast her eyes on the contents of the vast room. There was nothing there except multi-hued machines and lights. Had such colourful lights been available the previous year during her sister's marriage, she would have made all the trees in her garden glimmer. The very next moment she felt repelled by the lights that kept pricking her eyes. She felt like running to a window to lean out. She kept scanning the walls, but found no opening. She started running here and there, searching for an opening to escape. Finally, exhausted, she sat down. She hid her face in her hands and began to sob. The five statues stared at her in amazement. After a while one of them went near her. He/she held a pocket radio-like gadget near the girl's head. She began to drift into an artificial calm.

She was again stretched out on a bed. All the five formed a circle and seemed to get into a discussion. Their museums contained many skeletons of ancient humans and their artifacts. But they were seeing for the first time a living, walking, talking girl!

The girl again got up. Now she seemed calmer. One of the five came and stood close to her. The girl observed the person closely, but could not determine whether the person was a male or a female. The person extended an arm to give to her something that looked like a shining golden plate. She gathered up courage and took it. And immediately she began to comprehend the sequence of events that brought her there.

Her name was Ahalya Verma. Originally she was from the state of Uttar Pradesh but she had gone to Mumbai for studies. She was studying microbiology at Elphinstone College. On June 15, 1984, she had started out with ten companions from Bombay Central station to conquer Everest. Ahalya was fully trained in mountain climbing. The leader of the team was Mr. Pavankumar Khachar. Pavankumar was completely at home in every nook and corner of the Himalayas. All the year round he lived in the lap of the Himalayas. Ahalya was journeying to the Himalayas for the third time, but she was in even higher spirits this time because of Pavankumar's presence in the expedition.

The first six days of the ascent of Everest went without trouble. On the seventh day the sherpas warned the team not to proceed further. The sherpas lived in the Himalayas and knew every pulse of the royal range. Ramsing Sherpa was the most experienced of all the sherpas and all such expeditions preferred to take him along. Ramsing advised against going further. But Pavankumar over-ruled him on the strength of his own experience. For climbing the next peak it was necessary to descend 500 feet to a valley and then resume climbing. Pavankumar also noticed the faint shadows of a storm rolling in from the distant horizon, but he thought that it would be possible to reach the camp in the valley before the storm struck. There were good facilities there, and besides, the storm's fury might be less in the valley. The team, therefore, moved forward quickly in the belief that it would be able to reach the camp site in the valley before the storm.

They had covered three—quarters of the way. Now only three miles remained. Suddenly the storm approached like a huge invading army. It engulfed the entire sky. The eyes got totally immobilized in the rampaging storm. The deadly cold wind could peel off the skin. It was accompanied by raging, swinging snowfall. The snow was slapping the face with the power of a wrestler. The team began a retreat. For half an hour the members could keep in touch with each other through voice. But then all their voices were drowned in the roar of the sky. It became impossible to discern anyone else in the team. Soon it became virtually impossible to keep one's feet on the ground, so terrible was the force of the hurricane. Ahalya was catapulted twice into the air. She clung to the ground. She hid her face in her lap to keep warm. She coiled up her body as much as she could and turned into a ball. She hoped to conserve heat and avoid the blows of the ice on her face. She was conscious of the faint beat of her ebbing life. Her loved ones crowded into her memory. As her mind began to get cloudy, she began to seek the images of her parents. Her memory could not quite hold their entire form. She could not remember what happened after this.

Then her heart stopped and consciousness shut down. And finally, layers of snow piled up on her body, and Ahalya was buried in the Himalayas. She awoke again after a thousand years.

Two lives in one! Life enters the same body a second time and the frozen body again starts functioning! Ahalya got so excited with this thought that she let off a cry of joy that reverberated in the entire lab. The scientists, used to the quiet of a cemetery, were stunned. For a moment they became deaf. The same fate befell the viewers of the screens. These people had more or less forgotten how to vocalize, and so they were simply dazed by the cry. As was usual with her, she shouted as if she was the leader: "Say, hip-hip-hurray for Ahalya!" Ahalya shouted thrice but the lips of the others standing there remained sealed.

Ahalya felt quite upset because she thought these people were deliberately humiliating her. While shouting hip-hip-hurray, Ahalya had put the golden plate on the floor. A scientist quickly put it back into her hand. Now Ahalya realized that these people were not trying to insult her;

they just could not make the noises she could. Ahalya went to a person standing close to her, took out her tongue, and started twisting and turning it. What a long tongue she had! With ease she could touch the tip of her nose. With her two hands planted on her waist, and her tongue dancing in all directions, Ahalya made a grand tour of all those standing there. Then she approached one of them and said, "Why don't you at least open your mouth?" She repeatedly demonstrated how the mouth could be opened. After much struggle, like a rusty box being opened after many years, the scientist opened the mouth. Ahalya barely had time to glimpse the tongue before the mouth was again shut.

Ahalya was delighted that these persons were at least trying hard to do what she wanted them to do. All her remaining diffidence vanished. Her natural exuberance, suppressed out of fear, now re-surfaced. By turn she got each of the five to open the mouth. She made each repeatedly take the tongue out. But the mouth barely opened and the tongue could barely be seen. Then she tried to make them say "Uh . . . uh", but in vain. Ahalya wondered: "What sort of people are these? They cannot speak, they cannot understand speech!" They could grasp Ahalya's thoughts with the help of the golden plate, but not her speech. She was amused by the 'progress' of these people! She thanked the Lord that she was born in another era.

Then Ahalya started playing a new game with the five. She formed a lotus with her fingers. She asked them to imitate her. Their inflexible fingers bent but barely. The effort on both sides continued for a long time; but the result was zero. Ahalya remembered her hostel. She remembered the limbless beggar squatting near the gates of the hostel. He would beg, shaking the stumps of his arms. She used to tremble at the sight. The hands of all these five had fingers and yet they seemed to have shed their fingers and turned their palms into stumps. A tremor flitted through her body. Crimson lines of pain creased her face. Her eyes filled with tears. "Please stop my heart . . . I don't want to live here", Ahalya sobbed.

None of the five could understand what Ahalya was doing. This was beyond their empathy, and so none could console Ahalya. Ahalya remembered home. The picture of how upset her parents got when they saw her crying arose in her mind. Ahalya was an expert at taking offence, and her father at pacifying her. Her sobs got more convulsive as she remembered her parents.

Ahalya's eyes got swollen from crying. Her face turned red. Sobbing, she said loudly, "I am hungry." She began to think of her favourite dishes: mango ice cream, dal-bati, rabadi, kofta curry, pulao of peas, jalebi! A robot came to her and delivered a pill. Ahalya felt revulsion for these people. She thought: a pill for dinner, a pill for quenching thirst, a pill to satisfy every want, and to satisfy any remaining desires, the gadgets—Lord! To live here one needs no eyes, ears, nose, or skin. Like the tail, slowly these people will lose all their sense organs. There will remain just a shining log of intelligence!

The pangs of hunger began to create an orchestra in her stomach. To satisfy it, with regret Ahalya put the pill in her mouth. The hunger just vanished!

One of the five came nearer. With the help of the golden plate, the person signaled Ahalya to follow. Ahalya complied. She remembered her childhood train journey. She remembered the song 'Comes the forest, comes the thicket, the train skips over rivers and rivulets'. Here, it was: 'Comes a structure, comes another structure; in the structure's glitter the sight melts'! Everywhere there were gadgets, gadgets, and gadgets. And the fanciest gadget was Man!

The person was noiselessly sliding along. Ahalya had to run to keep pace. In between Ahalya would get so tired that she would sit down. The person would also stop. Once, the person tried to catch Ahalya's arm. But Ahalya started screaming. She was mortified—what if she got burnt alive by the aura surrounding the person. They traveled quite a distance. There were no clocks, and so it was not possible to measure time as Ahalya knew it. There was neither night nor day there. Ahalya recalled her mornings: tender dawn, splashing pink. As soon as it arrived, the birds would start warbling. A pink vim would pour into earth's every particle. Morning prayers would commence in the temple on the hill-top. When the scorching noon struck twelve one wondered whether the gentle evening would ever come! The evening's russet melted into the night. Like the spots of a bandhani, stars stitched their light on the sable night. And amongst them glowed the huge full moon.

Ahalya sat down to recover from fatigue. Her eyes began to wander. She felt suffocated by this tortoise shell-like structure and these humans undergoing life-imprisonment in it. In frustration she asked the person standing next to her, "How do you spend time here?"

The person began to transmit thoughts to Ahalya. "For many years now, man has colonized the planets of the solar system and nearby stars. We are playing an active part in the development of all these civilizations. We have greatly developed the science of peace. My colleagues and I are expert peace scientists. We have established complete peace on the Earth. We carefully monitor distant human populations, lest man's destructive instinct again rears up and destroys him and his civilization! Whenever we notice any disturbance in any part of space, we get there with our peace-restoring machine. We radiate peace waves in all directions and envelope the entire planet in peace. To be able to reach the farthest parts of the settled universe, we have developed extremely fast vehicles. They are powered by radiation energy. Some of us are space vehicle experts. Several of our people are engaged in the production of space vessels.

"We have complete knowledge of our bodies. Here, no disease is incurable. We put on this light-shield to protect ourselves. Even bacteria and viruses cannot penetrate this shield. Experts here prepare spare parts and replacements for every organ of the body.

"We change our structures as per our need. We have highly proficient architects and physicists for doing this. Humans here are produced only in laboratories. We take the human from the laboratory only after the person has developed psychologically and physically to the point where the person can take responsibility for his or her physical and mental development. Two of my four colleagues are administering our life-development centre. We spend our whole life in scientific study and our self-related work."

Ahalya was dazzled by the progress these people had made. But she also scoffed at their mission of marching ahead bearing the flag of science. Without saying a word she covered her eyes with her hands and kept sitting—and dozed off.

Ahalya could not keep count of the days—for there was neither day nor night nor calendar there. But the main new development was that she felt that two of the five scientists were attracted to her! Ahalya sensed some competition between them in walking with her, in being close to her. For the first time Ahalya felt a human sensibility in the two that earlier had seemed to her to be non-human. One day one of them even mildly pushed the other behind and communicated to Ahalya that she should walk with him! In the eyes of the other person Ahalya saw a dim gleam of anger. Ahalya felt elated at receiving so much attention. She was convinced that these two were males and the other three were females.

The man alongside her began to slide. He held Ahalya's hand. Ahalya also began to slide with him. For some reason Ahalya lost her fear of the light—shield. His touch, though, was not that of any human she had known. She could not compare his touch with any other touch. He kept looking at Ahalya. For the first time there Ahalya turned into a dancing wave of delight. She remembered the childhood story of magic sandals. She started laughing loudly and excitedly. Seeing Ahalya happy, her companion also seemed to become happy—his lips parted slightly in a smile. Perhaps this was an illusion. But Ahalya bloomed with pleasure.

In a few moments both entered a habitat museum. They came to the section where relics of a thousand years ago were kept. In the entrance itself there were many clumps of trees—mango, banyan, peepal, gulmohur. Ahalya felt as if she had entered a jungle. She started chattering like a bird. Soon came fields of different sorts of grain. Seeing a yellow field of mustard she remembered her family's farm in her village. She badly wanted to cuddle the plants. She ran and caught a shrub in her fingers. But she got a shock, as if the shrub had stabbed her. Everything there was lifeless! Everything stored there as a record of the past was artificial.

With a voice choking with emotion, Ahalya told her companion, "I want to see the green canopy of a living tree. I want to hear the calls of birds. I want to roll in green grass. I want to live among people like me. I want to go home!"

The man began to converse with her telepathically. "You are a thousand years old. Your 'home' is no more."

"But take me at least to the seashore! I want to put my feet in the shifting, sliding sand. I want to see a clump of coconut palms with their fronds dancing in the wind."
"I don't understand what you are saying!"
"You people are living dead. Don't you ever feel like seeing flowers and leaves and trees and birds?"
"We have often seen these in museums. But what is there to see in them?"
"Do you like to see me?"
"Yes."
"Why?"
"I don't know."
"Do you enjoy looking at the skeleton of a girl kept in a museum?"
"No."
"You *would* enjoy nature if ever you have dipped your feet in the waters of a real sea. If you have heard a bird call *then* your eyes would chase it, is it not? Why don't you just stop my heart? I have no stomach for this sort of a barren life."

Anyone watching Ahalya plead with her two folded palms for a mercy killing, would have melted with pity. Something touched this non-human human. He kept staring at her. Ahalya saw frozen emotion thaw in the depths of his eyes.

People watch Ahalya insatiably on their screens. Somehow they all love to see her. They flock to see her wandering in the city structure. Everything else seems pale in comparison. These days the intellectual—scientific odyssey seems to have slowed here a little. Many feel a little jealous of the five scientists. They feel that they have appropriated Ahalya. They, too, want to see her from close, touch her.

Often Ahalya goes out of the city's mammoth structure to watch the sky. But she gets little pleasure in watching this sky. It is just not like her sky. It is full of the trails of flying machines. Watching these machines, she is reminded of a face full of small pox scabs. She feels that these lights are leaving burn-scars on the beautiful body of the sky. If only these lights, vehicles, people disappeared for a moment, she could see 'her' sky.

Viewing the barren land outside the city structure revolts her. And yet it is earth, real earth. Sometimes she rolls weeping on the ground. She scratches the soil with her nails. She scoops out a handful and brings it inside the city structure. She mixes water in it, and makes different toys. She makes small beads of earth and bakes them in a kiln. After much search, she has found tinted earth, and she makes colours out of it. With these she paints the beads.

When one day she was shown on the screen threading the beads into a necklace, the viewers were entranced by the stylish way she held the beads and nimbly manipulated her fingers for threading them. When she finished the necklace and put it on she became so happy that she started singing and dancing. A millennium younger human caused the hearts of her millennium older viewers to flutter.

Ahalya's spirit is inundating the structure's arteries like a torrent. The people here are beginning to get swept along. Four of the five scientists are against showing Ahalya on the screen. They feel that she will destroy their civilization, which has reached the zenith of science. But one of them is convinced that the sole remedy for their diseased culture is Ahalya.

Now Ahalya is able to differentiate among the five scientists that earlier appeared to her to be cast from one mould. One of the five has become an intimate friend. They feel warmth in each other's company. They can understand each other even without the intercession of the golden plate. Only Ahlaya can understand what her friend speaks because it is so garbled that it would sound to the people of her time just rolling, tumbling gibberish. Even so, for a man who could not even utter ah or uh, this is a signal achievement. Ahalya has moved mountains to teach him this much. Nor is the friend's learning effort any less.

One day Ahalya was adamant: "You'll have to call me Ahalya." Her friend's tongue would crawl up like a spider but slip down a letter. Finally his tongue began to remain steady, even if feebly, on a few syllables: A-LA-LA. Ahalya began to leap around like the lit up waters of the fountains of Vrindavan Gardens. Her friend kept on tirelessly uttering ALA ALA, as if invoking within him some mysterious power.

Finally Ahalya said, "Enough, enough! Stop your ALA. Now you tell me what I should call you."
"My number is 9000560005800123456789l", he communicated.

Ahalya laughed and laughed, holding her stomach. Then she said with seriousness, "How drab you all are. Even after catching hold of delight you remain drab."
"Am I like what I was earlier? I can hear you. I can even understand you a little."
"Let us find a name for you that exudes the fragrance of your personality." She snapped her fingers: "Found it, found it!" Ahalya skipped about in glee. Her friend stared at her in wonderment.

"I will henceforth call you Rama."

Ahalya kept chanting "Rama, Rama, Rama Rama!"

The freshly denominated person was attracted by the feeling bubbling in the intonation. He had never experienced this feeling while communicating any one's number. He liked his new name. He began to repeat his appellation again and again, like a child who has just learnt a new word. But his articulation was still babble.

Rama was the first person there with a name. When the next day Rama and Ahalya called each other on the screen by their names, the viewers beamed with joy. Then began a great fad of opening the mouth and making sounds.

All the four scientists began to get annoyed with Rama, and for three main reasons. First, Rama often desired being alone with Ahalya and thus they felt left out. Second, it was unpardonable that a front ranking scientist like Rama should imitate an ancient, primitive ape-like female, and induce others to do so! And then, despite considering Ahalya primitive, all four were attracted to her. They began to boycott Rama. They told Rama, "Please separate your work from ours since for some reason your values have changed from ours." The very next day Rama and Ahalya started their independent research project.

Ahalya and Rama were no longer shown on the screen. Instead there were again programmes of scientific progress. People felt that Ahalya was forcibly taken away from them. There were meetings and discussions. Representatives took their bombshell of a protest and met the four scientists.

The four scientists told them, "Don't you remember the nuclear war a thousand years ago? Man destroyed civilization and himself with the 'your'-'mine'-jealousy-revenge poison. Only a few survived. They saved themselves with their scientific proficiency. They decided that they would create a new culture from which this poison of possessiveness, rivalry, and selfishness would be excluded. They cloned many humans who were peace loving. They diminished the sexual attraction between man and woman. From then on to-date mankind has lived in total peace. Science is the perfect truth, and if we relinquish it, our end will be near. There is dissension amongst us because of Ahalya. Her association with us will lead to our destruction."

The scientists communicated their message in silence, but the people, not heeding it, kept on chanting Ahalya's name.

The scientists decided to explain the situation to Ahalya herself. From the Earth's safety viewpoint they requested Ahalya to depart with Rama to some other place. Ahalya requested some time to think over this request.

Rama's sensibilities are blossoming, and with that he is also establishing scientific milestones in his laboratory. Rama is training Ahalya's mind in various ways. Nowadays the two are engaged in a major invention. They are making a machine with which a person can experience every moment from birth to death stored in Ahalya's mind, as vividly as Ahalya herself.

After a heroic effort that amazing machine was now ready. Ahalya met all the four scientists. At first they refused to experience her life with the help of the machine. Ahalya said, "I like all of you peace loving people very much. It was not possible to be rid off man's lower nature without scientific prowess. Have I not experienced man's cruelty, violence, and deceit? I had always thought that if man becomes peaceful the world would turn into a heaven. This became possible through science. But you have totally surrendered yourselves to science. Along with cruelty, violence and deceit, science has also sucked out your sensibility! It has taken away pleasure with pain."

They did not appear to understand her. Again and again Ahalya pleaded with them to experience her life with the help of the machine. Two female scientists were persuaded. They thought, "We do not have to become like Ahalya. What harm is there in once experiencing her life?" They persuaded the other two scientists.

Ahalya attached tiny plugs on the heads of the scientists. Then she began to transmit to them special, emotionally charged episodes of her life. Now all the four are Ahalya:

Little Ahalya has tucked herself into a corner of her mother's sari. Ma is gently caressing her with her silken palm. Pappa asks her fondly, "Where has Ahalya gone, where has she gone?" "Here I am, here I am," chirps Ahalya, peeping from Ma's sari. Pappa clasps her to his bosom and then tosses her high in the air. The laughing-screaming Ahalya keeps bouncing up and down like a ball in Pappa's hands. Ma and Pappa clasp Ahalya so many times to their breasts, their leaping hearts beat in unison . . . !

From a crack in the door, the sun flows in like a yellow waterfall. Little Ahalya, flailing her arms, jumps to catch in her small fists the numberless shining particles streaming like the stars of the Milky Way. Then arrive two sparrows to bathe in this yellow waterfall. Ahalya's dark eyes fly everywhere, chasing the flapping wings of the sparrows. Suddenly, a green caterpillar, held in the beak of a sparrow, falls down. Ahalya goes near the caterpillar, sees it slithering on its stomach. Seeing the crawling bright green colour, she starts clapping. She tries to catch it with her fingers . . . .

Gopal is sitting next to Ahalya on the bench in the classroom. He asks her, "What is it that one can see but not touch?" Ahalya gives many answers, "The moon; the sun; the sky . . .". Gopal keeps shaking his head. Finally he says, "Ramaben's braids." Ahalya's eyes shine with mischief. She raises her finger to ask whether she can go out for a drink of water. On returning, she lightly touches the teacher's braids from behind the teacher. The whole class bursts into laughter . . . .

With one string of braided hair in front and another behind, Ahalya is pacing leisurely in the college's corridor. She has come in a little early that day. She becomes aware of some one following her. She turns her head, arches here eyebrows like a bow, and shoots a gaze at the footsteps following her. On seeing Anil, her face turns pink, as if a red tide has surged inside Ahalya. Anil comes very close and stands almost touching her. There are sparks, as from the rubbing together of two flints . . . lightning flashes in all of Ahalya's pores . . . .

The four scientists experienced many such incidents of Ahalya's life. For a while they were stunned by the intensity of these experiences. Then all four began to communicate with one another. One of them opined that from now on only such humans should be created that not only are peace-loving but also capable of loving others intensely. The remaining three agreed.

Another scientist opined that they should cast away the light-shield and explore the world outside the city structure. Rama took the lead by casting away his light-shield. For Rama this was not new. He had touched Ahalya several times without the light-shield. All the four cast away their light-shields and ran outside the structure. All four held each other's hands. They experienced a faint electric current pulsing under their skin. But even in this feeble touch they experienced a pleasure never before experienced.

All four sat on the ground under the open sky. They started throwing fistfuls of earth on one another. Sounds started tumbling out of their mouths from the uncontrollable ecstasy they were experiencing. They started passing fingers over their own and others' faces. How the fingers relished ascending the nasal mountain, or playing on the wet lips!

All four scientists felt that the rest of the people should have the same experiences they had. They put this idea into practice with the help of Ahalya's machine. Every human was able to enter into Ahalya's emotional world. Thus sprouted tiny, green shoots of sensitivity.

The face of the city structure has undergone a change as if a fairy's wand has passed over it. The magic wand is not a fairy's but Ahalya's. Now this city looks attractive. It stands amidst a forest of green trees. There are multi-coloured flowerbeds set in emerald grass. The air resounds with the calls of birds. Flocks of peacocks lounge on the gates of the city. Far away, deer can be seen roaming in the fields. Holding pearly seed, golden ears of corn are swaying in the fields. Men and women resemble butterflies in their variegated clothing. Azure gleams in the birds' flapping wings. Small houses surround the city structure. One can hear calls of endearment. People are busy doing their work in the laboratories, schools, and workshops within the structure.

Today there is a great festival. Ahalya has given birth to a boy. The baby is seen on the screen moving its tiny limbs about, crying with its mouth open. The entire city is transfixed watching this. This is the first human not to be engineered in the laboratory. He is the essence of the human of a thousand years earlier and a thousand years since.